WRIGLEY SANDERS

Born in the Bleachers

A NOVEL

MARK SCARPACI

Copyright © 2015 by Mark Scarpaci. All rights reserved. No part of this publication may be reproduced, distributed, or transmitted in any form or by any means, including photocopying, recording, or other electronic or mechanical methods, without the prior written permission of the author, except in the case of brief quotations embodied in critical reviews and certain other noncommercial uses permitted by copyright law.

ISBN: 978-1-48359-919-9 (print)
ISBN: 978-1-48359-920-5 (ebook)

For my son Tate.

The events in this book happened sometime before November 2nd, 2016.

"It's Cubs' baseball. Anything can happen."
– Connor Kelly

CHAPTER 1

"It's been one heck of a game, folks," drawled Vin Scully in the Wrigley Field booth. "Here we are, tied in the top of the 13th, and the Cubs desperately need some outs. After blowing their third lead in as many an inning, the Cubs are down to their last pitcher, a little-known rookie named Wrigley Sanders."

Wrigley, startled by the phone ringing in the Cubs' bullpen, looked up at the bullpen coach.

"Sanders!" yelled Les Harris, "Warm it up!"

Wrigley moved out to the bullpen mound and started to throw, easy at first, relaxing into the act, forgetting about all else around him, looking for his pinpoint control. Once loose, he fired it up a little, just to hear the pop of his catcher's glove.

"You might be asking yourself," Vin Scully said, "how does a kid born legally blind and nearly deaf, end up pitching in the World Series for the Cubbies? Well, years ago, his parents were at Wrigley when an Astros center fielder stroked a fly ball over the left field fence. It was a dandy. Wrigley's dad reached up to catch it and missed it by an inch. It was a costly error because the ball hit his wife smack dab in the belly. Thing is, she was eight and a half months pregnant, went into labor, and before you could say, 'bring in the lefty,' Wrigley Sanders was born."

All warmed up, Wrigley looked up at the sky. "Papa," he said under his breath to his deceased Grandpa Connor, "I hope you're seeing this…"

He took a number of deep breaths, each time slowly letting out the air and emitting a low, long, soft "paa paa" sound. It was a deep-breathing exercise his mom had taught him that always helped him to relax.

"Hey Wrigs," called out Rudy "Toothpick" Jones from the shadows. "I can see you're nice and loose. Good work."

Wrigley slowly turned around. "Aren't you supposed to be in the dugout?" he said.

Wrigley's pitching coach stepped into the sunlight wearing a well-pressed Cubbie uniform. He seemed to be gliding toward Wrigley with his smooth gait and trademark smile. The tall, skinny black man with the fleck of gray in his jet-black beard was just the man Wrigley needed to bring him back to the moment.

"Just wanted to wish you luck. I'm proud of how hard you worked. Never gave up. Try to enjoy the moment. You deserve this," Toothpick said.

"Thanks, Coach," Wrigley said. "You know, Mom said I'd be a closer…"

"I know," Toothpick smiled, "I know."

Then, after a long pause and a bit more seriously, Toothpick said, "Remember: forget your eyes, Wrigley," tapping Wrigley's horned-rimmed glasses before moving his boney finger to Wrigley's chest. "Pitch with your heart. That's where you shine."

Wrigley wanted to hug him but was close enough to see Toothpick's samurai glare that stopped him in his tracks.

"And remember: load, relax, release," Toothpick said.

"Yup, just like outfield fly-fishing," Wrigley said with a smile, remembering the day Toothpick had him use a fly pole to perfect his accuracy.

On cue, Tom Petty's *Don't Back Down* blasted loud enough that Wrigley thought about adjusting his state-of-the-art micro-hearing aid, but much to his pleasure, the 4200 model made the adjustment for him. Wrigley smiled. It was nice to hear his song loud and clear.

"Your mom would be proud of you," said Toothpick, backing toward the dugout, then under his breath, "Here we go, Wrigley, here we go."

With a couple of claps, Toothpick seemed to disappear as if into Ray Kinsella's cornfield.

Wrigley took a big breath, raised his chin, cracked the kinks out of his 33-year-old neck, stood tall, and began his jog toward the mound. A squat five foot eight and weighing 205 pounds, he was so plump that his belly wiggled over his belt buckle as he jogged. His feet pointed outward, giving his movement the distinct impression of a huge, dark-haired duck waddling toward the mound. His curly, black hair was so thick it strayed out of his hat and literally floated his grey and black vintage Cubs road cap—a style last worn by the team that won the 1908 World Series.

He arrived at a gorgeously manicured mound, obviously cared for by a fanatic just like his Grandpa Connor, who used to groom the Cubbies' field during spring training. Every detail was perfect—not a pebble on the smooth, red dirt. He thought about how his grandpa had always told him, "It's Cubs' baseball. Anything can happen." He smiled, then picked up the rosin bag, chucked it in the air a couple times, and peeked toward the left-field bleachers.

★ ★ ★

"You can be anyone you want to be," Annie Sanders whispered as she patted her huge, pregnant belly. It was a beautiful, sunny Sunday afternoon at Wrigley Field, and despite being eight-and-a-half months pregnant, there was Annie, sitting with her husband, Bert, in the left field bleachers, the air redolent of a mix of stale beer, ballpark franks, and peanuts nearly as salty as the bums that surrounded her. There was no place she'd rather be, especially on *this* day, for *this* doubleheader. The Cubs were on a run. This was *the year!*

The Astros were up, and pitcher J. R. Richards got off a lucky swing and put a good charge on the ball. It continued to race toward the left field bleachers—directly toward Annie. Caressing her unborn baby, Annie was oblivious to the crack of the bat and the scorched line drive coming in her direction.

But Bert, baseball glove in hand, tracked the ball over the fence and reached out just in the nick of time to…miss it entirely. The ball hit Annie squarely in the belly with a loud *thump*.

"Oh my god! Oh my god!" Bert said as the surrounding crowd stood by in silence staring at Annie's belly, paralyzed about what to do and morbidly curious to see what would happen.

But Annie was calm, shaking her head to get out the cobwebs and rubbing her belly. She offered a smile and said, "I'm all right," as she turned her attention to the runner rounding the bases. "Oh, c'mon!" she said, extending her arms to the field in disgust—looking uncomfortably like Don Zimmer. "Where's the ball?" She glanced around and caught sight of it near Bert's feet. "Give me that!" she ordered.

Still shaking from the potential consequences of his big E, Bert grabbed the ball and handed it to her. With great effort, Annie stood up, held the ball high for everyone to see, dramatically turned to the north, then the south, the east, and west, and powerfully tossed the ball back out onto the field.

"Take *that*, you son of a bitch!" Annie yelled.

The bleacher bums leapt to their feet, cheering the gesture of protest. The Cubs' left fielder picked it up, looked around confused, and motioned to throw it back. Annie led the section of fans, broadly waving their arms that they didn't want it, so he shrugged his shoulders and tossed the ball back toward the third base side of the field. The bleacher crowd cheered even louder.

With her now-famous toss, Annie had started a new tradition at Wrigley Field. To this day, when a visiting team hits a home run, the ball is tossed back onto the field.

"Hear that, son," Annie said, looking down to her belly, "they're cheering for *you*." And with that, she suddenly felt dizzy and passed out.

"Annie?" said Bert, shaking her by the arm. "Annie!"

"Sir," interrupted an older gentleman with a well-worn black bag sporting a crinkled Cubs stick-on logo, "please let me through. I'm a doctor." The doctor waved some smelling salts under Annie's nose. Startled, she came to in seconds.

"There you go," said the doc. "Where'd the ball hit you?"

Annie pointed to the right side of her belly. The doctor gently put his hand on the spot of contact.

"How's that feel?" the doctor asked.

"Okay," Annie said, seeming unsure. As the doctor turned to grab his stethoscope from his bag, Annie grabbed the middle of her belly, reacting to a sharp pain. The doctor quickly put his hand where she held hers. "Normal contractions," he said, smiling, but within a few minutes, the contractions were coming on stronger. "I'll be right back," the doctor said calmly. He went over to one of the ushers. "Call the paramedics—*now*." He came back to Annie and noticed a wet puddle below her.

"My water broke," Annie said.

"Sure seems that way," the doctor said calmly with a smile.

"Does that mean she's having the baby now?" Bert moaned nervously.

Positioning Bert behind Annie, the doctor put his left hand on Bert's shoulder, looked him straight in the eyes and motioned with his other hand for him to zip his lips. A few Cubs ushers were milling about near the top of the stairs waiting for the paramedics to arrive, but they were nowhere to be found. Annie started to breathe heavier and heavier, puffing like an aging, over-the-hill pitcher trying to turn his only single of the year into a double.

"Hew, hew, hew, hew, hew, owh," she puffed during each contraction, which were now just 30 seconds apart. "I should have watched this game at home," said Annie, looking a little regretfully into the doctor's kind eyes. He returned the look with a comforting smile.

"It's okay," he said. "I've delivered babies in the middle of a blizzard on Lake Shore Drive. Why not on a sunny day at Wrigley? Now, go ahead…"

Annie nodded yes and instinctively started to push. The crowd had actually cleared a little space for her, putting down stadium pads. A couple of large, tattooed sailors stood guard facing the field with their baseball mitts, in case of yet another home run. They didn't trust Bert's glove.

Sweat poured off Annie's forehead. Bert paced behind the doctor, pissed that he'd been shushed. A seemingly adult-sized left hand with long, slender fingers slowly came out. The doctor had never seen fingers this long before. Then the rest of the baby came halfway out, headfirst—blue-hued with the umbilical cord wrapped around its neck, silent. The doctor knew he had to act fast.

He gently tugged the baby all the way out, swiftly removed the cord from around the baby's neck and cut it.

"A boy!" the doctor said. The crowd roared with delight.

The doctor gently tapped the boy, hoping for a cry. Smacking him a little harder, he finally got one. Annie blew a big sigh of relief, as the doctor gently put the baby on her chest.

The nearest Cubs usher couldn't help himself. "What you gonna call him?" he asked Annie.

"Bert Junior!" Bert said excitedly.

"Nope," said Annie, looking Bert right in the eyes, "Wrigley."

Bert's smile turned into a confused stutter—"But, but…"

"He's going to be a closer for the Cubs," Annie said to anyone who would listen, "gonna help them win a World Series."

The usher smiled as he scribbled Wrigley Sanders on a small notepad. He scurried to the broadcast booth, tore off the piece of paper and handed it to the public announcer, Andrew Belleson. Andrew took the paper, covered his mic and mouthed, "What's this?"

The usher pointed to the left field bleachers and gestured a round belly, a constipated facial expression, and a cooing smile as he looked down at his arms, which were rocking an imaginary baby. Andrew's confusion morphed into a wide-eyed grin. "Folks," he said excitedly into the mic, "we have a new Cubbie fan just born in the left field bleachers. His name is—Wrigley Sanders."

Finally, the paramedics arrived and Annie was rushed off to St. Joseph's Hospital. Wrigley spent over a week in the hospital fighting for his life, with the rear right part of his head damaged by the impact of the ball. When he was deemed in the clear, the doctor said he would most likely have some disabilities but that right now it was hard to predict.

"Wrigley is the toughest baby I've ever seen in 30 years of practice," said Dr. Hallihan, looking at Bert with what Bert took to be chastisement. "By all rights, he shouldn't be here right now."

Burt looked down at the offending hands that failed to make the big play. "We're still not sure about his eyesight and we know he doesn't hear so well, but he's a fighter and time will tell. Let's keep an eye on that soft spot."

"Thanks, Doc. You saved a Cubbie fan." Annie said, looking down at Wrigley.

"My pleasure," said Dr. Hallihan, smiling down at Wrigley. "*Especially* if he's a Cubs fans.

Bert raised his eyes from the floor and caught a glimpse of himself in the hallway mirror. Ragged and worn out from the events of a long week, he did a double take, because he swore he saw a huge black E, which he surmised stood for error, staring right back at him on his forehead.

CHAPTER 2

Toothpick, trotting out to the mound, found Wrigley staring out to left field. He tapped Wrigley on the shoulder, startling him. "Wrigley, you okay?"

Wrigley looked at him like they had just become acquainted. He'd been staring at the exact spot where he was born, and he could swear that he'd seen his mom in the crowd. The thing was, she was deceased.

Toothpick scrutinized his eyes like a parent trying to assess if his child is under the influence. "We need you, man," said Toothpick, as he grabbed the ball out of Wrigley's glove then slammed it back in so hard it shocked Wrigley back into focus.

"I got this," Wrigley responded with a confident smile, still peeking at the bleachers. Then to Toothpick, "I'm good. Why not, right?"

Toothpick just shook his head with a smile and left the mound. On the big screen, over 35,000 fans saw a huge image of Wrigley as he smiled widely, his crooked teeth on full display.

Vin Scully drawled, "There he is in living color, folks. Wrigley Sanders, who with a little help from his eye doctors beat all the odds and made it to the majors. Oh yes, and did I mention Wrigley pitches with both arms?"

Wrigley began to warm up left handed, and after a while, he used his specially designed ambidextrous glove to switch hands. He threw a single right-handed pitch and the umpire jumped up, raised his hands, and quickly trotted out to the mound.

"You going to switch it up during the game?" the umpire asked.

"Yup," Wrigley said.

"Pick a side at the beginning of each batter. Once you touch the rubber, that's it. Then you and the batter, if you want, get to change once during the at bat, after your first pitch. Got it?"

"Yes, sir," Wrigley said.

★ ★ ★

"Yo, Christian, can yous take offt da haddt during da anthem," yelled the buff, shirtless, tattooed Boston Red Sox fan baking in the 98 degree heat and 100 percent humidity at Wrigley Field.

Annie, wearing a Cubs' blue muumuu, struggled past the man and sat down in the left field bleachers. She had gained over one hundred pounds since Wrigley's birth nine years before. Maybe it was the stress of Wrigley's medical issues, or perhaps it was just living with—or more aptly, *without*—Bert.

Right now, Annie was just glad to be spending time with her dad.

Connor Kelly, a big, strong, redheaded Irishman pushing 70 finished off his fourth beer with a huge gulp and a burp. He was carefully pacing himself at one every two innings. In the old days, when he hung out with Mr. Wrigley himself on Catalina Island, there was no pace, except a fast one.

"Wrigley seems to be doing pretty good," Connor said.

"Ah, I don't know," said Annie. "He still doesn't have a lot of friends. I think he'd be better off in regular school, but they won't take him."

"It's criminal," Connor said.

"He has Bozo's Circus and the Cubs," said Annie. "He throws every day—like clockwork. Says he's going to take the Cubbies to the World Series."

"Nothing wrong with that, Annie girl," Connor said. "A kid should dream. And remember the story of Mordecai 'Three Finger' Brown…"

Annie nodded and smiled. "How could I forget? How many times did you tell me *that* one?" she said, looking back to the field. "Whattaya think, Pops? Think we can pull this one out? We're only down by a run."

"It's not over," he said in his best imitation of Yogi Berra, Annie sarcastically chiming in, " 'til it's over.' I know, I know."

Connor looked at the scoreboard, a massive steel structure that took a crew of three to run. Wrigley Field always took him back to his golden years when he worked for the Wrigley family in California. Those were the days. He loved that the Cubs still raised a white flag with a large blue W for win, even if that meant continuing the tradition of a blue flag with an L if they lost.

Just then, the first hitter for the Cubs lined a single to left field. Annie and Connor both leaned forward. The next hitter blasted a ground ball through the hole toward Annie and Connor for a single.

"It's gettin' interesting," said Connor, glancing over at Annie.

"Wrigley? Wrigley, get over here!" yelled Annie as she waved to him.

Wrigley, who was running around in his Cubbie gear chatting with the other "bleacher bums," as he pored over his *Baseball Prospectus*, cocked his head, adjusted his hearing aid, and realizing it was his mom, wandered over to her with his distinctive duck-like waddle. At nine, he was a short, chunky kid, with coke-bottle glasses, a pair of huge hearing aids that hung over his ears like saddle bags (and let him hear most things okay if he focused), and thick black curly hair that sat on his head like a poodle's.

"You catching this?" Annie asked.

"Of course," Wrigley said, rolling his eyes.

"Two on, two out," said Connor to himself more than to his grandson.

Connor eyed Annie as the Cubs' shortstop drew a walk. Now it was bases loaded, and up came a little-used pinch hitter, Adam Korn.

"Oh no," Wrigley groaned. "This bum's not even battin' his weight."

"Keep the faith, Wrigley," Connor chuckled at his grandson's sass. "It's Cubs' baseball. Anything can happen."

"We'll see, Papa. We'll see," Wrigley said as he tossed a baseball high in the air, his long fingers wrapping the ball and twisting it with ease.

The count went to zero and two, then, on an ill-advised fastball right down the middle of the plate, the hitter smacked the ball down the right field line. In came the first runner, then, as the runner on second rounded third, the whole crowd in the left field bleachers—Annie, Conner, and Wrigley included—flailed their arms toward home like the excited third-base coach. As the runner crossed the plate, well ahead of a desperate relay throw, the crowd collectively leapt into the air.

The Red Sox's manager slammed his hat to the ground as 39,242 Cubs celebrated their victory and gazed up as the white flag with the big blue W was raised high in the sky for everyone to see.

An hour later, back at Annie's house on Kenmore Street, Annie finished preparing Wrigley's birthday dinner, while Connor looked at a crayon-written paragraph on the refrigerator door.

The Important Thing about Me
The important thing about me is that I am a baseball player. I like to fish. I like Bozo's Circus. But the important thing about me is that I am a baseball player.
Wrigley Sanders – 4th Grade

"Well, he knows what's important in life," said Connor as Annie brushed by with a plate of hot dogs and he reached out to snag one.

"No, no, no," Annie laughed, slapping Connor's hand away. "Wait till we sit down."

As Annie put a big crock of baked beans on the table, completing Wrigley's favorite meal of ballpark frank 'n' beans, she called out to the man of the hour, "Get it while it's hot!"

"So," Connor said smugly, "is *Bert* going to make it?"

Annie looked up at Connor—her expression betrayed that the answer was, as was typical, "not likely," but that she was still trying to hide Bert's irresponsible behavior from Wrigley.

On cue, Wrigley entered the kitchen and beheld the happy sight. "Can we wait for Dad?" his eyes darting between Annie and Connor.

"Sure, honey," Annie said, stealing a glance at the clock then nodding at her dad. "We'll give him a few more minutes." She covered the steaming hot dog plate with tinfoil and the pot of beans with its lid.

Connor rolled his eyes and opened his hands to the sky, expressing his disapproval. But Wrigley smiled and ran out of the room, probably back to his *Baseball Prospectus*.

Half an hour later, Annie called out, "Wrigley!"

Wrigley ran back into the kitchen, and not seeing his dad, looked up at her inquisitively, like he was willing to wait forever. "Looks like Dad has to work late. Let's eat. Maybe he'll be able to join us for cake." She knew it was a long shot but hoped Bert might at least half deliver. Wrigley shrugged his shoulders, obviously disappointed, and sat down at the table, his face lighting up a little as he lifted the lid off the pot of beans.

"How about a game of catch?" Connor said after dinner, playing his part in stalling birthday cake.

"I'll get the mitts!" Wrigley said, running off to his room.

"Where is he?" Connor whispered. Rubbing his left shoulder, which seemed to be bugging him lately. "When he gets here, I'm gonna take him out back and do a little dental work." Connor felt a jab in the center of his chest.

"Dad, you okay?" Annie asked.

Connor shook his head "fine" as he rubbed his chest one last time and said, "Who doesn't show up for their own kid's birthday?"

"We need to get you back to the doc and see…" Annie started to say, stopping as Wrigley came running into the kitchen, holding an orange-colored catcher's glove, a righty glove, and a lefty glove.

"Let's go, Papa!" Wrigley said.

Connor smiled at Annie and nodded as if to say "I'm okay" and then went over to a canvas bag he had brought in earlier and pulled out a brand new baseball glove. Over the years, he had taught Wrigley to pitch with both arms. They started so young, Wrigley didn't think much of it. So normally, he used two gloves—one lefty, one righty—changing mitts each time Connor called out a right or left handed batter. This glove was different.

"Happy birthday!" Connor said. "This new-fangled 'ambi-glove' lets you switch from your left to your right, and it was made just for *you*."

Wrigley gazed at the brown leather glove with awe. "Papa" he said, transfixed, "it's *beautiful*."

"A special glove for a special young man," Connor said, his chest feeling better.

Connor put the glove on his right hand and patted it with his left, then switched hands and gave it one solid pop with his right.

"Here, give it a try," Connor said. "It may be a little big, but you'll grow into it."

Wrigley put the glove on and switched it back and forth, over and over again.

"That's incredible," Annie said to Connor. "How'd you…?"

"No biggie," Connor said to Annie with mock nonchalance. "Had a friend who knew a guy."

Wrigley slowly looked the glove over and noticed a Cubs logo. Then he saw his name embroidered right along the side.

"Wrigley Sanders," he said to no one in particular, "just like the pros. Wow!"

"Come on, kid," Connor laughed, flashing Annie a big smile, "Let's see what you got." And they were out the kitchen door.

Out back, Wrigley stood about 30 feet from Connor and tossed the ball back and forth, warming up his arm.

"Okay," said Connor, waving for Wrigley to back up. Connor crouched down into a catcher's position. "What you throwing these days?"

"I've been practicing Sandy Koufax's heater."

Connor smiled. "That-a boy!"

Wrigley eyed an imaginary batter and then went into an elaborate windup that coincidentally looked exactly like Sandy Koufax's. He drew back his left arm and unleashed a straight-as-an-arrow, 45-mile-per-hour fastball that thumped directly in the catcher's mitt.

"Who-wee!" Connor said. "You got it down kid! I think I'm gonna start calling you Sandy K…or maybe Sandy for short. Okay, let's see if you can strike somebody out."

"Sure," Wrigley grinned. He knew what was coming next. Grandpa liked to announce while Wrigley pitched.

"Now batting, the world's best all-time hitter, Babe Ruth. But folks, on the mound is the great Sandy K," Connor said in his very best announcer voice.

Wrigley wound up and threw a heater.

"Strike one!" said Connor, raising his right arm into the air. "The Babe looks to the dugout for help, but not even his momma is gonna save him from the great Sandy Sanders!"

Wrigley giggled. He loved it when Papa announced. Wrigley did the exact same windup over and over, while Connor announced a full inning.

Ruth, Gehrig, Crosetti—all went down on strikes. Side retired, Connor stood to give his creaky knees a break. "I see you really have been studying those films I gave you."

"*Of course,* Papa!" Wrigley responded, re-stating the obvious.

Connor smiled. "You know, it doesn't matter if your eyes aren't perfect or if you don't hear so great. A lot of ball players made it to the Bigs with bad ears or poor eyesight. The Babe had 20/200 vision in his left eye."

"Wow. I didn't know that," Wrigley said. Then looking down at his glove, "Thanks for the glove. It's awesome."

"Sure enough, Sandy."

He liked the new nickname. *Loved* it. Wrigley had spent hours watching the films his grandpa had given him. The films profiled some of the greatest pitchers of all time, but it was Sandy Koufax's motion that stuck. Every little move that the great Sandy made, he imitated.

Wrigley and Connor came back into the kitchen and saw Annie on the phone.

"That's a bogus excuse," she said angrily, then turned to see the boys coming in, flashed a fake smile and tried to shift into a kinder tone that was more like an angry whisper. "Fine, Bert. We'll see you when you get here." She hung up the phone and turned to Wrigley. She squatted down and put her hands on his shoulders. "Dad got held up," she said, dropping her eyes. "He can't make it."

Annie lit the nine candles atop the three-layer chocolate cake with the Cubs logo as she and Connor sang "Happy Birthday." They ate the cake in relative silence, Wrigley clearly disappointed, but occasionally looking up to smile to let Connor and Annie know he was okay. They weren't fooled.

"How 'bout a bedtime story, Sandy?" said Connor as the three of them sat there with empty plates. Well, at least two were empty. Wrigley had taken a few bites and just picked at the rest. "Go get your PJs on and brush your teeth. I'll be right there."

Wrigley half-smiled, got up from the table, and left the kitchen. Annie eyed her dad.

"I'm fine. We'll talk later, Annie girl," said Connor, patting Annie's hand and standing up.

"Thanks, Pop," she said.

Connor sat on the edge of Wrigley's bed, staring at a giant illustrated poster of Orval Overall, one of the Cubs' finest pitchers from the early days. Overall stood on a flat mound with green grass in the background and a pink horizon behind him. No stands or fence in sight.

He wore a Chicago Nationals uniform with black hiked up socks, grey pants and top, black belt with matching shoes, and short mitt—with a white, long-sleeved undershirt. He was a right-hander in mid-windup looking toward home. The poster had a posed, surreal old-time feel that to Connor seemed magical.

"Overall, what a pitcher," Connor said to Wrigley.

"Still my favorite, Papa," Wrigley said, sitting up in his Cubs pajamas, snuggled under his Cubs comforter, in his blue and white room.

"You know who mine is?" Connor asked.

Wrigley shook his head "no."

"Ever heard of Toothpick Jones?" Connor asked.

"Nope. Why'd they call him that?"

"That's what I'm gonna tell ya," Connor said. "You see, Toothpick was black, and back in his day, in 1955, no black player had ever pitched a no-hitter in the modern day big leagues. His real name was Sam Jones, and he had a curveball that would break at least four feet. If you were a right-handed hitter, the ball would come from behind you, then break clear across the plate—nearly impossible to hit."

"Cool!" said Wrigley, "I should study his pitch."

"I would," said Connor. "So in '55, Toothpick was pitching for the Cubs, and…"

"Wait, wait, wait, Papa," Wrigley said. He wiggled out of his sheets and cuddled around his grandpa. "I love Cubbie stories."

"Okay, Wrigs," Connor said with a smile, cuddling with his grandson.

"So, the announcer was a guy named Harry Creighton, and he told Sam Jones, who liked to keep a toothpick in his mouth, that if he threw a no-hitter, he'd give him a toothpick made of gold."

"Gold?" Wrigley said.

"That's right, Wrigs, *gold*. And for Sam, that was incentive enough. So every day, he went out and tried to pitch a no-hitter. He had one going too, all the way until the 9th inning. But in the 9th, he walked the first three batters. Now, some people say he walked those men on purpose, which many have a hard time believing, and some say he didn't, but what happened next was a miracle."

Wrigley leaned in closer.

"With the bases loaded, Sam looked up at Harry the announcer, gave him a confident smile, and held up the okay sign to Harry like he was in complete control—after walking three batters in a row."

A pain shot through Connor's chest. He felt a bead of sweat form on his forehead. This time the pain didn't go away. He wiped the sweat, looked at Wrigley and smiled. Wrigley felt his grandpa jolt, but when he saw him smile, he smiled back and asked, "Can you finish the story Papa?"

"Maybe tomorrow, Wrigs," Connor said, moving away from Wrigley to the edge of the bed. He felt like a knife had penetrated his left shoulder blade. He actually turned, wondering what was going on. His chest became tight, like a giant nutcracker was crushing his ribs.

"Goodnight, Wrigs," he managed to say as he stood up, pale, getting short of breath, sweat now dripping off his forehead. "I love you."

"Goodnight, Papa," Wrigley said, a little confused at his grandpa's behavior.

Connor leaned down and gently put both hands on Wrigley's shoulders. "Wrigley. Promise me something. Promise me you'll follow your dreams. You wanna pitch for the Cubbies—you do that. Remember, in baseball, in life, anything can happen. Your chance will come, Wrigs, and when it does, promise me you'll give it your best."

"Sure, Papa," Wrigley said. While his grandpa could be a bit goofy, Wrigley saw that he was being serious—and expecting a serious response. "I will, I promise."

Annie came to the door, smiling, but seeing Connor's sweaty face, grabbed him by the waist and led him out.

"I love you, Wrigs," Connor spat out through the pain.

"Wrigley, tuck yourself in," Annie said, trying to stay calm. "I'll take care of Papa."

In the living room, Connor collapsed into a chair.

"Oh, shit," Annie said. She ran for the phone and dialed 911.

Connor grabbed his chest and let out a whispery, "Marilyn," as he slowly fell out of the chair facedown onto the living room carpet.

"Yes. 168," Annie said, having taken her eyes off Connor for just a second. She saw Connor out of the corner of her eyes on the floor, dropped the phone and ran to him.

"No, no, *Dad*!" Annie yelled. She rolled him over and tried to hold her shaking hands onto the side of his neck. It was nearly impossible. She didn't feel a pulse. The color had run out of his face. She started to sob and frantically pressed on his chest but didn't know CPR.

"Mom?" Wrigley stood in his Cubs jammies in the hallway, rubbing his eyes.

"Oh god," Annie said, looking down to her dad, then over to Wrigley without his glasses on. She knew he couldn't see much.

"Papa, you okay?" Wrigley asked, squinting to see.

"He'll be…" Annie said pressing faster on his chest. "Damn," she said, not knowing how fast to go.

"Go to the phone, Wrigley. Operator, *help*!"

She pressed a few more times and then took a look at her dad. His face had turned a light, chalky grey. His eyes, wide open, had a tint of yellow. He was gone. She could feel it. She went over to Wrigley by the phone and gave him a big hug.

"Papa loved you, Wrigs. He did."

The operator's voice could be faintly heard from the phone, "Hello? Are you still there?"

Wrigley let out a small gasp and started crying. Annie hung onto him. He was shaking. Then he stopped breathing, turned red, then a little blue.

"Breathe, Wrigley. Just Breathe," Annie said as calmly as she could muster.

Wrigley took in a jagged breath, and then let it out, saying "Paa paa."

"Good Wrigs. Just keep that up. Take your time. It's gonna be okay. Big breath!"

Wrigley took in an even bigger breath, this time letting it out even slower, emitting a low, guttural "paa paa" that seemed to last for a whole minute.

CHAPTER 3

Wrigley glanced at the opposing dugout and saw the number seven hitter warming up. He felt something deep down inside his gut snap.

"What the heck?" Wrigley said, bending over in pain. He had blown out his belly button many years back and had had an operation, but this was a different kind of pain, deeper. He quickly surmised it was his body telling him he wanted to face the very best.

Wrigley knew he had to listen to his gut. He settled in, pitching right handed, and proceeded to walk the first batter in five pitches, and walked the second batter in four. The Cubbies' manager, with a knot in his stomach, turned to Rudy "Toothpick" Jones, the son of Cubs pitcher Sam "Toothpick."

"You know this kid, right?" the manager moaned. "Talk to him."

Toothpick slowly meandered out to the mound, hopping over the third base chalk line for good luck.

"Really?" Toothpick softly said when he arrived at the mound.

"Why not?" Wrigley said. "It worked for your dad."

Toothpick shook his head, looked at the ground, and just smiled, "Now Wrigley…"

★ ★ ★

It was May 12, 1955 during a Cubs/Pirates game when Cubs pitcher Sam "Toothpick" Jones walked Gene Freese, Preston Ward, and Tom Saffell to begin the 9th inning. Yup, he was Toothpick's dad and he had a lot on the line. TV announcer Harry Creighton had told Sam he'd give him a toothpick made out of gold if he pitched a no hitter. So here stood Sam, winning four to nothing in the 9th, and after walking three men in a row, he looked up into the announcer's box and smiled at Harry, holding up his hand with the okay sign.

Then, he proceeded to strike out the first batter, Dick Groat, who got caught looking at his patented curveball. Sam's curve would start behind a right-handed hitter and break a full four feet right over the plate. No matter how hard the batter tried to stay in the box, they had to bail.

Sam wiped the sweat off his brow. If he could pull off this no hitter, he'd be the first black pitcher in the modern era to throw one. His catcher came to the mound and tried to talk him into pitching for a double play ball.

"No," Sam firmly said, "I haven't come this far to not strike out the side."

The next two Pirates were no lightweights. One of them was none other than Roberto Clemente, who, even though he was young, would be no small feat to strike out. Still, Sam got Roberto to swing through a pitch and strike out, and now the only thing stopping Sam from making history was this last hitter.

The announcers were talking about history in the making, and the Cubs' defenders felt the pressure to perform. They didn't want to blow a play and ruin Sam's historic no-hitter. Artie Gore, the umpire behind the plate, had never seen anything like this, and neither had the mere 2,918 Cubs fans that were now on their feet, begging for a no-no. Sam cracked a smile up to Harry in the press box, threw an amazing curveball that caught the last hitter looking—strike three. Sam "Toothpick" Jones had won his bet by delivering on his promise of a no-hitter!

★ ★ ★

"You could get pulled?" said Toothpick.

"Tell him I walked them on purpose," Wrigley said.

Toothpick shrugged and said, "He's going to think you've lost your mind."

Toothpick walked back toward the manager, struggling not to crack a smile.

"Says he's got it under control," Toothpick told the manager.

"Yeah. Well, I'm pulling him if he doesn't throw a strike," the manager said, his neck and face matching the red in his Cubs' logo. "I bet Gonzalez can throw."

"Perhaps," Toothpick said, hiding his grin. Sure, on a lucky day the outfielder Gonzalez might throw a strike, but a meatball that would get hit out of the park. No, he was stuck with Wrigley.

Wrigley did throw a strike—an inside one—then four more balls, on purpose. The booing became so loud it drowned out the public announcer's attempt to introduce the next hitter.

Out of the corner of his eye, Wrigley caught the outline of Carl, the young "blind kid" that he'd met his first day at Wrigley Field and given words of encouragement to. His whole family was there, all wearing custom-made Cubs shirts with the word "Sanders" across the back, even the grumpy dad. Carl was pointing to the back of his jersey, a big smile on his face.

"What is he doing out there?" the red-faced manager yelled. "Why is he so happy? That's it. I'm pulling him," he said to Toothpick, then briskly moved toward the mound.

"I'm sorry son. You loaded the bases. Give me the ball," the manager said. Wrigley kept the ball in his mitt.

"This is the World Series," the manager said. "Give it to me!" Wrigley just smiled as the manager held out his hand.

"Well, folks," drawled Vin Scully. "Seems Wrigley Sanders isn't happy about getting the hook. Pretty rough way for a rookie to break into the big leagues. But in this game, you don't get the outs, the party's over. Wouldn't you like to know what he's saying to his manager right about now?"

"Coach, I can't," Wrigley said. "There's nobody else who can throw. Theo has been saving me for this very moment. Pull me now you lose. Let me pitch, you win. You know I have pinpoint control, with both arms. I walked those three men on purpose."

"Wha…why would you do a stupid thing like that?" the manager moaned.

"I'm not worried. My mom said I'd win this game."

"Seriously?" the manager said, taking his hat off, rubbing the sweat off his bald head, and shooting a glance at Toothpick, who could only smile back. "Your mom?"

"Yep," Wrigley said, looking him right in the eyes. "I got this. Let me do my job."

After a long moment, the manager put on his hat, took a slow deep breath, and said, "Okay. Do me a favor. Give me the ball. I'll rub it up and hand it back. That way I don't look like a complete idiot out here. You better know what the hell you're doing."

Wrigley gave him the ball and the manager rubbed it with his hands, thought about keeping it, then tossed it back. "Go get 'em," he said, and jogged off with a fake smile, muttering through gritted teeth, "'My mommy said…' We're screwed."

★ ★ ★

The morning after Connor's death, Annie woke up to a loud rhythmic pounding coming from Wrigley's room. She opened his door to find her recently turned nine-year-old boy sitting up in bed rocking back and forth, slamming the back of his head against the bed board.

He wore his new glove, popping his hand hard into the pocket, then switching glove sides and popping the other hand. His eyes were bloodshot, his hearing aids out, glasses off. His black, bushy hair looked like a bird's nest swaying in a windstorm. Annie motioned for Wrigley to put in his hearing aids. He did.

"You okay, sweetie?" Annie asked, knowing he clearly wasn't. She didn't know what else to say. He just kept rocking and popping his glove. Left, right, left, right.

"Papa was right, you know," Annie said, as she put a pillow behind his head. "You're special."

"Promised him I'd pitch for the Cubs," Wrigley said, pounding his fist into his mitt one final time, putting on his glasses, then getting up to turn on his black-and-white Super-8 projector. "Gonna watch some film."

Annie placed her hand on his leg and gave it a squeeze before leaving Wrigley to his Zen. Wrigley stayed in his room with the old-time pitchers all day and then all night for four straight days, barely sleeping and not eating. He pounded his new glove over and over until his hands became red and a little raw.

On the fifth day, Annie rolled up the Orval Overall poster above Wrigley's bed. It was the last thing to leave Wrigley's room. Everything they could fit into Annie's old red station wagon was packed and ready to go. She'd made a decision to leave Bert and now had a destination—Connor's home in Los Angeles.

"They have a lot more options for you out West," Annie said, hoping Wrigley was on board. "And you can play baseball year round. I think you'll like it, Wrigs. I really do."

Wrigley just sat there, apparently too numb to weigh in. Annie pulled out of the driveway, heading right toward Wrigley Field. They had lived in its shadow on Kenmore Street, and their home had served them well. She drove without direction, absentmindedly. Wrigley, rocking back and forth and popping his mitt, looked out the window and softly asked, "Can we at least get cannoli?"

Annie's face broke into a smile. "Good idea, Wrigs!" She changed her direction and pulled up to the local deli.

"I'll wait here," Annie said, hoping Mr. G could cheer Wrigley up a bit.

Inside, Mr. Gaviglio saw Wrigley coming, held up a finger, and quickly whipped out a cannoli and put it on a small piece of waxed paper. "For my besta customer!"

"Thanks," Wrigley said. He averted his sad eyes downward, then looked up to Mr. G. "We're leaving for California. My grandpa died and he wanted us to live in his house."

"So sorry," Mr. G said, noticing Wrigley's red hands but deciding to leave it alone. He snapped his fingers. "Wait here!" Mr. G disappeared into the kitchen. When he returned, he came around from the counter and handed Wrigley a huge pink box of two dozen cannoli. "It's a long drive."

Wrigley's eyes became huge and filled with tears. He wrapped his arms around Mr. G, nearly crushing the box.

"Say 'hi' to your mama, and *buona fortuna!*"

"Holy cow!" said Annie as Wrigley climbed into his cushy den in the back seat. "Give me one of those!"

And off they went. Soon, Wrigley was asleep. After a few hours, Annie started daydreaming about Connor's last day of spring training on Catalina Island. He had told her the story years ago.

★ ★ ★

It was after a double-header, and Connor was finishing up his groundskeeper duties. He paused for a moment to watch the brilliant orange blaze drop below the clear blue Pacific Ocean. It was his 20th birthday and he didn't have a clue what he was going to be doing with the rest of his life. He had been offered a "real job" back in Chicago and had agreed to take it.

As the sun dipped below the water, a bright green flash went blip, then disappeared, leaving Connor leaning on his rake. He was about to finish his work when he heard a soft female voice, "Beautiful, isn't it?"

Startled, he turned to see a young, magnificently dressed, blond-haired woman, standing near the edge of the mound.

She giggled. "Sorry," she said, "didn't mean to scare you." Her perfect white teeth sparkled in the fast-approaching dusk, and she smelled like the tropical flowers that grew on the island. "I'm Marilyn," she said, holding out an elegant hand.

"C…C…Connor," he replied, taking her hand. "Connor Kelly. Pleased to meet you."

He held her hand in his a moment longer than was necessary. She blushed and said, "Isn't it beautiful?"

Connor looked at her curiously, his other hand gripping the handle of his rake.

"The field, I mean. The smell of the grass and all that…"

"Oh yeah, beautiful," Connor said.

"I *love* baseball," Marilyn continued.

He exhaled, "Wow. Really?"

Marilyn gave Connor a large sparkly smile.

"For the last three years, this is all I've lived for," Connor said, grandly waving the rake across the field. "I love it because—well, anything can happen. But as of tomorrow, it's all over for me."

"*All over*?" she asked curiously.

"Yep. I'd like to stay in baseball, but I gotta grow up, go back home to Chicago. I found a 'real' job."

"Why don't you stick with baseball if you love it?" Marilyn asked.

"I don't know. I'm 20. Today, actually, and I think I um…"

"It's your *birthday*?" she cut him off. Connor nodded.

"That was a nice birthday sunset," she said, waiting for Connor to respond, but he didn't.

"What are your plans?"

Connor took her in. She had a soft, easy smile, with just a peek of her pearly whites showing through. "I…ah…that's the problem. I don't have one, except Chicago," he said.

As he looked out onto the field, Marilyn realized he didn't understand the question.

"I mean for *tonight*, silly. It's your birthday. What are your plans for *tonight*?"

"I don't have a plan for tonight either," he said, embarrassed about the confusion.

"I think it's important to celebrate birthdays," she said. "Don't you agree? Wait, I have an idea! Let's go for a swim!"

★ ★ ★

The loud blast of a truck horn and bright headlights snapped Annie from her reverie. She quickly turned the wheel to the right, avoiding a huge 18-wheeler that had swerved to its right to avert disaster. Adrenaline pumping through her body, Annie quickly turned to Wrigley. "You okay, Wrigs?"

"What?" Wrigley said groggily, rubbing sleep from his eyes.

"Nothing," she said, "we're fine…we're fine." But she wasn't. She missed her dad, missed him badly. Wrigley was awake now. "Mom," he said, "how long till we get there?"

"Just getting started, Wrigs. How about a story? Ever hear about Merkle's Boner?"

Wrigley giggled. *Boner.*

Annie giggled back. "Back in September of 1908, which was the last year the Cubs won the World Series, they had the famous double-play combination of Tinkers, to Evers, to Chance, and your buddy Orval was throwing his curve, with his wide-sweeping motion and the little jerk at the end…"

"I can do that one!" he said.

"It's a beautiful windup!" Annie said. "All those guys teamed up to make a run for the pennant against the New York Giants. They played a really important game in late September. The winner was likely to go to the World Series. And with the game tied, bottom of the 9th, the Giants had men on first and third. Up comes Al Bridwell, who smacks a hit up the middle. The runner from third scores, so it's game over, right? But the Giants' runner at first, Fred Merkle, doesn't run to second."

"Wait a minute," Wrigley said. "They can still get him out and the run doesn't count."

"Exactly. But Al musta forgot that rule in all the excitement. Johnny Evers didn't because he called for the ball. Cubs center-fielder Solly Hofman threw it to third, where the Giants' Joe McGinnity, realizing what Evers was trying to do, grabbed the ball and threw it back into the outfield."

"No!" cried Wrigley. "No way!"

Annie looked in the mirror, nodding her head emphatically. "All the New Yorkers rushed onto their field, celebrating their win. But the Cubs' third baseman Harry Steinfeldt took the ball out of a fan's hands and fired it to Evers, who tagged second base for the force out. Frank Chance had escorted umpire Hank O' Day over to second base, explaining what had happened, and the runner was called out. The game was declared a tie."

"So the Cubs got to the World Series?" Wrigley asked.

"Not so fast," Annie slowly said. "At the end of the season, the Giants and the Cubs had the same record. So they played a tie-breaker in New York City, and the Cubs won and then went on to the World Series—and won it all, the last time they have ever done such a deed."

"I'm gonna take them there, Mom," Wrigley said. "You wait and see."

"I would love to see that, Wrigley." Annie said.

CHAPTER 4

The leadoff batter came up to the plate. Wrigley stared down into his glove, not looking at the hitter, trying to stay calm in this bases-loaded World Series moment. The catcher put down one finger for a fastball. It seemed like everything was moving way too quickly. Wrigley knew he had to think fast—Koufax or Ryan? He chose Ryan and stood tall, reared back with his right arm and threw his best imitation of a Nolan Ryan fastball, right down the pipe, letter high.

Smack. The ball came rushing right back at Wrigley with warp speed. He turned his body and got up a glove but it bounced off the back of his head—right on his soft spot. Fireworks exploded in Wrigley's brain. He buckled to his knees, found the ball on the ground, fired home missing the force out, then collapsed to the ground, holding his head.

"What the hell just happened?" the manager moaned. "He's done."

"Hold on," Toothpick said to the manager. "I got this..."

Play stopped. Toothpick and the trainer came running to the mound to check on Wrigley.

"You okay, son?" asked the trainer."

Wrigley tried to talk but no words came out of his mouth. Toothpick looked at the trainer, "Could you give us a moment here?" he said. The trainer nodded yes and jogged off the mound, waiting about 10 yards away.

"Did you hear the question?" Toothpick asked Wrigley.

Wrigley nodded yes.

"Are you okay?"

"I...have…to…be…" Wrigley responded, each word slowly following the next after a long gap. "I'm…all…we've…got."

"Shit," Toothpick whispered, waving the trainer back to the mound.

★ ★ ★

Annie pulled up to Connor's house in the dark. A warm, strong wind called the Santa Ana blew through four giant palm trees that Annie had helped Connor plant near his driveway so many years ago. She parked next to her dad's car and smiled at his "Cubs Fans Parking Only" sign. She looked back and saw Wrigley was sleeping.

"Come on, Wrigs," Annie said, shaking his leg gently.

She ushered him toward Connor's white-and-blue painted home, past his Cubs flag that flapped in the breeze near his front porch, into the guest room, where she gently placed the half-asleep Wrigley onto a dusty bed.

" 'Night, Wrigs," Annie said.

" 'Night," Wrigley mumbled and now fell fully asleep.

Annie walked out to the kitchen and looked at the walls. It never changed. As always, it was chock full of memories: dozens upon dozens of neatly framed pictures, most from her dad's days of working for the Cubs. She loved the photo of the West Coast Wrigley Field—a cozy venue in South Central L.A. that seated close to 20,000 fans. With its Spanish-style tiled roof, it had hosted Pacific Coast League games for years, even acting as the home park for the California Angels in 1961.

She giggled as she looked at the photo of folk hero/bank robber John Dillinger, from the 1930s, dressed as a postal worker, sneaking into Wrigley to watch a game without getting arrested. She still wondered who had taken the photo and how her father had come by it. She moved over to a black-and-white shot of Ernie Banks with his sunny smile. Ernie had written, "Connor, let's play two…rounds of golf." "Mr. Cub" was the first black Cub, and his number 14 the first ever retired by the Cubs organization. She turned and surveyed pictures of young Connor fishing in the blue waters off Catalina; of mountain goat rodeos and laughter; BBQs in front of the Wrigley mansion; and even a shot of Sam "Toothpick" Jones and Connor enjoying a beer during spring training. She got chills when her eyes landed on the shot of Connor and Marilyn at the beach with the words "Follow your dreams" scribbled in small script. Her dad had never said it, but she knew he felt he'd made a huge mistake not going to Arizona with the Cubs to pursue coaching when he was 20. And finally, she walked over to her favorite photo of herself. She was nineteen, tall and slender, standing near her horse with a huge smile on her face, the green hills of Malibu Canyon in the background.

"Those were the days," she said, catching her reflection in the frame window and recoiling at the juxtaposition. She moved over to the kitchen table and noticed an 8½ x 11 inch manila envelope with "Annie" written roughly across the whole surface in permanent marker. It was her dad's writing. She opened the envelope and read a typed note: "Annie, if you're reading this, then I'm gone. I know it's a shitty deal. I love you sweetie, and I'll miss you. Didn't want to go, but I guess there are some hitters in heaven who need advice on how to hit a curve. Or pitchers in hell who need advice on how to throw one. Make sure Wrigley gets his eyes fixed right away. I've enclosed a check that'll pay for it and a whole lot more. My investments with Mr. Wrigley paid off well. I know Wrigs is going to take my passing hard. If he doesn't start to mix with kids his own age pretty soon, he's going to remain our little guy forever. I know a part of you would love that. Me too, but it's just not right for him."

"I know, Pop. I know," Annie said through tear-filled eyes. Then she saw a handwritten part in the bottom of the corner that said, "Almost forgot. My long-time friend Rudy Jones has promised to get Wrigs a tryout with the Cubs when he's ready. 555-572-2355." Annie found the check under the note. She had never seen so many zeroes before. Wrigley was going to get the best for his eyes. Wrigley came shuffling out, rubbing his sleepy eyes.

"Wrigs, go back to sleep."

"Not tired, Mom. I need to watch some film," Wrigley said.

"Want some company?" Annie asked.

"Sure," said Wrigley, shrugging his shoulders.

Wrigley and Annie walked into Connor's den. The walls were covered with more pictures, mostly of baseball players, many of them famous, with hand-written notes: "Couldn't have made it to the show without you. Thanks Connor!" and "Your curve got me here…you da man!"

Annie turned on Connor's Super-8 projector, using the wall Connor had cleared off as the screen. Sandy Koufax blasted onto the wall.

"I know him," yelled Wrigley, squinting to see the image on the wall. "Sandy Koufax."

"Can you do his windup?" Annie asked innocently, full well knowing the answer.

"Oh, I can do it!" Wrigley said, suddenly excited. "Papa sent me this one." He popped his mitt right-handed, then left-handed, then getting up in the middle of the room and doing a perfect imitation of Sandy's windup, using his oversized fingers to put extra spin on the imaginary ball. Annie gave him a standing ovation and smiled. She then loaded more pitchers onto the screen.

Wrigley watched Juan Marichal's high kick that looked like he was either going to uncork a missile or fall backward off the mound. He awed at the way Gibson put so much body into every pitch, he'd fall toward first base. But what he liked most was Sandy Koufax, whose lefty delivery had so much extension it looked like he was doing the splits.

"See that, Wrigs?" Annie said during a close-up of Sandy Koufax's hands. "You have hands like Sandy." Sure enough, Sandy Koufax had the same long, thin fingers that allowed him to get that extra spin on his curveball. Annie looked at the screen and back to her son and realized that for the first time since Connor's death Wrigley was actually smiling.

"Wrigs, I have to hit the sack," Annie said, yawning. "You okay?"

"I'm gonna stay up a bit," looking to his mom with a smile to see if she approved.

"Enjoy," Annie said, caressing his cheek, glad to see him smile. "Love you."

"You too Ma," Wrigley said. As Wrigley went through a film of Nolan Ryan, he also saw some footage of Greg Maddux, a younger Cubbie that had won 18 games this year. As Wrigley watched many others Grandpa Connor had admired across several generations, the pop in his mitt became more relaxed. His arms loosened up and he began to imitate the pitchers' body movements with ease. Finally, he stumbled upon some footage of his favorite pitcher of all time, whom he'd never seen in action—Orval Overall. As the whir of the clicking projector droned on, he stood up, tried to imitate Overall's motion and broke out in spontaneous announcing, just like Connor used to do.

"Overall on the mound. Ruth at the plate," Wrigley said. He stopped, looked up to his Papa, pointed to him, just the way he had seen other pitchers and batters do when they were acknowledging a higher power and continued, squatting down like he was behind the plate.

"Behind the plate catching is Connor Sanders. He drops a signal for an Overall drop ball."

Wrigley put down four fingers, then turned and stood up like he was looking in for the sign and ready to pitch. "Orval catches the sign. Winds up. *Whooooooosh!* The drop ball strikes him out!"

Wrigley pumped his arm. He was so lost in the elation that he got lightheaded. The bed looked so inviting, he pointed one more time to the ceiling, to Papa Connor, and tucked himself in, a big toothy grin on his face.

CHAPTER 5

"Well, folks," said Scully. "Just when you think you've seen it all, this wonderful game of baseball delivers yet another twist. That ball came back so fast it could have killed Wrigley Sanders. He took quite a blow to his head, but Toothpick Jones and the trainer have him up and walking around, like a punch-drunk boxer on the ropes that just won't go down.

"How about smelling salts?" Toothpick asked the trainer.

"It might help," he said, going to his bag and retrieving some salt to hold under Wrigley's nose. Toothpick was careful to come in close and hover over Wrigley to block the TV cameras as much as he could.

★ ★ ★

Four years after his first consultation with Dr. Alan Harrison, one of the best eye specialists in Los Angeles, Wrigley had the operation. Annie had scheduled Wrigley's first consultation with Dr. Harrison the morning after their arrival in L.A., but Dr. Harrison, while optimistic about what might be accomplished— saying that with an operation and thick glasses, Wrigley might be able to achieve "normal" vision— urged them to let Wrigley's eyes develop into adolescence. After four annual check-ups, he finally deemed Wrigley ready.

Annie was the first one to see Wrigley. She entered his recovery room to find him fast asleep in bed. The lights were low and the TV was on. A Buddy Holly movie played on the screen. Something about Buddy's bold black frame glasses and aw shucks smile relaxed her. But it was just an actor *playing* Buddy Holly—that guy whose name she couldn't remember from that movie about the kid with the broken arm who became the Cubs' ace pitcher. It was on the tip of her tongue, when in walked Dr. Harrison.

"The procedure went well," Doctor Harrison said. "I think with prescription glasses he's going to see almost as well as most people."

Annie turned and smiled, holding back the urge to hug the good doctor and stuck out her hand. "Thanks, Doc. Thank you so much."

Dr. Harrison shook her hand gently and smiled a comforting smile. "You're most welcome." With that, he glanced down at his watch, and said, "Well, I have another surgery." Then, nodding toward Wrigley, he whispered, "You might want to let him sleep a bit more."

"Of course, of course, Doc," she whispered back, "thanks." With that, Dr. Harrison offered one last nod and exited the room.

Annie walked over to Wrigley and stared down at his face. She was surprised to see that he didn't have any bandages on his eyes. She rarely saw him without his glasses on now. At thirteen, he was becoming a young man, and she couldn't help but caress his cheek. Her stomach grumbled. She decided to get a bite to eat. As she exited the room, she took one last look at the television.

"Gary Busey!" she said, snapping her fingers, then, hearing Wrigley stir, she whipped around.

Feeling guilty about her outburst, she motioned with open hands toward Wrigley, like she was trying to magically coax a baby back to sleep. Wrigley mumbled something then turned his head in the other direction. Content he was still in la la land, she left the room, smirking. *Gary Busey.*

Just minutes after Annie left, though, Wrigley blinked open his eyes and the image on the TV screen came in to focus. Gary Busey was singing. Wrigley furrowed his brow, and sat up in bed, still not sure if this was a dream. What was Chet Steadman doing singing on TV? He blinked a few times, and as never before, could make out details, like Buddy Holly's glasses: dark, horned-rimmed wonders.

"That's it!" he said out loud.

★ ★ ★

A few weeks after the operation, Wrigley, with his brand new Buddy Holly corrective lenses, tossed a baseball in the air while he ate at the kitchen table at home. He loved that he could see the seams of the ball, and would blink rapidly so that he could see the stitches. It was a miracle.

"Wrigley, I think you need to get out of the house," Annie interrupted. "What teenager sits around all day watching baseball films?" Wrigley looked at his mom like she was nuts, "What teenagers *wouldn't* want to?"

"Okay," Annie said, rolling her eyes to the ceiling, exasperated. "But you need to actually *throw* those pitches, to real life frien…I mean, *teammates.* "

Wrigley stopped tossing the ball in the air and looked down at his plate like he was processing what his mother had just said. She had a point. "I think you might be right, Mom. Let's get on that. I'm gonna go watch some more film. Can I please be excused?"

Annie shook her head a little in frustration. "Sure, Wrigs," she said, glad he was open to the idea but aware of the task at hand.

She reached down, searching for the number to call the Santino family who lived catty-corner to Connor's house. She had made a casual friend in the mom, Regina. They had shared coffee a few times and talked kids. Connor had left her number in his letter. *Where was that letter?*, she thought, *as she riffled through the drawer.* Her mind floated back over the past four years and how quickly time had flown by. Wrigley had pretty much settled into school, a happy loner, content on watching every Cubbies game, studying his pitching films and playing catch with Annie. She had had to make some adjustments to life as a single mom, but it was worth it. Not having Bert in her day-to-day life had been a godsend. She seemed to have so much more energy when he wasn't around complaining about his bad lot in life. She finally found the letter, looked down to the number, and dialed it.

"Um…Regina," Annie said a little nervously, "I need a favor. I was wondering if Biggs could come hang with Wrigley. Maybe introduce him to some of the kids on the block? He's all healed up from his eye operation, and well, he needs to get out of the house. Maybe throw a baseball more…" She could hear all the commotion in the background. The Santino family had eight kids, all boys. It was a noise Annie knew well, having grown up with five brothers.

"Yes, of course," Regina said over the racket. "I know that one. I'm sure Biggs would be glad to come by."

"Thanks. You're an angel."

The next morning fourteen-year-old Joe "Biggs" Santino came to Annie's door. He stood six foot two and one hundred and twenty pounds. Tall, slender, with long brown hair down to his shoulders, dark skin, and a prominent Roman nose, he looked like he was cut out of a teen idol magazine, nervous as he was. He didn't want to be there.

Connor wasn't particularly welcoming to the neighborhood kids over the years, and ever since that Halloween when he had found Biggs' mischief-making friends hiding in the bushes, grabbed them by the ears, forced them to stomp out the flaming shit bomb they had left for him on his doormat, punctuating the lesson with "And if I *ever* catch you around my porch again [many swear words ending in] kill you," Biggs had stayed as far away as possible.

"Come on in," Annie smiled, then whispered, "Thanks for bringing your mitt."

Annie struck Biggs as a little gruff, but her genuine smile was disarming. He gingerly stepped into the Sanders household and beheld the shrine. Never had he seen so many pictures of baseball players in his life. Dozens he recognized and others he'd never heard of, but most were clearly from the old days—all of them signed, with handwritten notes to "Connor." It was what he imagined the walls of Cooperstown looked like, except this was more impressive. The ornery old man must be some sort of legend.

"Wrigley's in his room," said Annie, unable to interrupt Biggs' reverie. She smiled at his lack of reaction and then said, more to herself, "I'll get him."

Wow, thought Biggs, *that's Marilyn Monroe!* He knew her likeness from those pictures his grandma showed him of Joe DiMaggio with the movie star.

Annie returned without Wrigley. "He may need a little prodding, Biggs. He's just not sure. Doesn't have many friends." Then to herself, "*Any*, actually..." She caught herself; it was probably the wrong thing to say. "Can you reassure him?"

"Sure," said Biggs, newly restored. Annie's face lit up.

Biggs entered the room and was hit by another tidal wave. Everything—from the comforter to the sheets, the alarm clock to the pictures on the wall—had something to do with the Chicago Cubs. Wrigley was still in bed, gently rocking back and forth hitting his head on a pillow and popping his mitt.

"Hey Wrigley, I'm Biggs. You a…" Biggs couldn't believe he was asking this question, "…*Cubs* fan?"

"Yup," Wrigley said a little surprised, like Biggs had read his mind. Each boy didn't quite understand the other's reaction, but Wrigley, taking a few deep breaths and letting them out with a long, slow "paa paa," slowly stopped the rocking, then the popping, while Biggs just stood in awe, wondering what the heck Wrigley was doing.

Finally, after Wrigley settled down, Biggs said, "My grandma loves the Cubbies."

"You serious?" Wrigley started to smile. "In *Dodger* land?"

As Wrigley stood up from his bed, Biggs noticed Wrigley's feet pointed outward, "ducky style," revealing a good 30 pounds of extra flesh on his stocky body. His dark, curly hair was uncombed and disheveled, and his Buddy Holly frames with extra thick glasses sat on his face uneven and crooked. After not so subtly looking him up and down, Biggs asked, "Wanna play some catch?"

Wrigley's face started to brighten, but just as quickly, he averted his eyes downward. "Nah, thanks."

"You sure?" Biggs asked, shrugging his shoulders and looking at Annie as she showed up at the door.

"I just…" Wrigley started, "I'm not quite used to my new glasses yet."

"Oh! Okay," Biggs said. "Maybe some other time."

"Why don't you show Biggs Sandy's windup?" Annie chimed in.

Wrigley started to brighten again. Biggs looked confused.

"Wanna see something?" asked Wrigley.

"Sure," Biggs shrugged.

Wrigley turned on the black and white Sandy Koufax film on the old projector and sat back down on his bed. Up came the great Sandy, his movement fluid and expansive, unlike anything Biggs had seen before. Biggs wasn't sure if it was the tick, tick, tick of the black and white film, or just Wrigley's mesmerizing face staring at the screen, but he was all in. He sat on the bed, wondering why Wrigley was showing this to him, wondering what he had gotten himself into—but completely transfixed.

"That's one beautiful windup," Biggs finally said.

"Classic," Wrigley said, still mesmerized by a film he had spent countless hours watching, and now, with his new eyes, he was seeing even more incredible details. Biggs looked at Sandy, then looked at Wrigley and smiled. He liked this kid.

"Hey, you two," Annie said, peeking her head back into the bedroom. "Want some lunch?"

"No thanks. I probably need to go," Biggs said.

"But wait. Wait!" Wrigley said. "We have to watch Marichal…and Paige…"

"I'd love to," Biggs smiled. Then, rolling his eyes, "But I have some chores to do. Mom said I only had an hour."

As he walked out of Wrigley's bedroom, Biggs noticed a small, empty box that read "Cavaretta's" on the floor by his Cubs laundry hamper. He chuckled. "Later, Wrigley," said Biggs, giving him a half wave. Annie showed Biggs to the front door. "Come again?" Annie said, unable to hide the hope in her voice.

"Yeah, sure," he replied, not sure why Annie looked like she was about to cry. "Thanks, Mrs. Sanders."

★ ★ ★

"He's about my age," Biggs said to his mom upon returning home. "His room looks like it hasn't changed since he was 9. All Cubs stuff. Bubbs would love this guy. But he's shy and seems kinda sad. I got the feeling he didn't really want me there."

"When he lost his Grandpa, he went into a tailspin," Regina said, putting her hand on his shoulder. "Don't take it personally."

"I'm not done trying, Mom. I mean, he's actually a pretty cool kid," he said, looking at her like she was the one giving up. Then he smiled. "I have an idea though!"

Starting the next day, and for the next two weeks, Biggs dropped a small box of Cavaretta's cannoli on Wrigley's front porch. And each day he came back, the previous day's box was gone.

"I don't know who would do that," Wrigley told Annie when she inquired about the cannoli. Annie was a little suspicious that Wrigley was somehow responsible for fattening her up.

"I can't keep eating one of those a day," said Annie, only half joking, "It's gonna kill me!"

"Then don't eat it!" Wrigley said, hands on his hips giving his mom a chastising mug.

"Watch it, mister," Annie said, putting her hands on *her* hips and staring Wrigley down with equal mock disdain. "You *know* I can't do that!"

The two laughed, but an awkward moment passed between them, as what lay beneath was something darker.

When Annie was young, her five older brothers used to fight. All out *brawl!* They'd go down to the basement after tying one on and fight for the fun of it. Tough, young Irishmen with large, meaty fists, even the winner would wind up with a new mark, a crooked nose, or miraculously, a straighter one.

"Scram!" Annie's brothers would yell at her, and she would bolt from the little corner where she had built a fort for her and her stuffed animals and rush upstairs. She would go right to the fridge, grab a box of cannoli, and sit with it at the top of the stairs, hating the noise of fists on flesh and her brothers' cursing but feeling like she had to be on watch in case something *really* bad happened. She'd sit eating cannoli at warp speed, hoping Mom would come home soon. Though Mom worked three jobs, she was still a more hopeful prospect than Dad, who had problems of his own. Drinking, sure—the boys didn't get it from nowhere—but *baseball*. During baseball season, he was mostly to be seen at the Nisei Lounge. He'd often come home in time to tell the boys to "knock it off" and coax Annie—who had passed out at the top of the stairs, unfinished cannoli in hand—to bed. If the Cubbies won, he'd be a happy drunk, recounting the game's best moments; if they lost, he'd pour his heart out about lost dreams—"I had a better curveball than *Pasual!*"—and the stresses of raising six children. This only made Annie crave cannoli more. Fortunately or unfortunately, there was always a box or two in the fridge—eggs, milk, and cannoli were the foundation of the family shopping list.

Annie had shared this story with Wrigley one night not long after their arrival in L.A. She stayed strong for Wrigley by day, but after he went to bed at night, she would sit in the kitchen, head in hands, bawling her eyes out. One evening, she turned to see Wrigley at the kitchen entrance, watching her, pale as a ghost. She frantically reached for the tissues, but realizing she had been caught red-eyed, just smiled and patted the seat next to her, inviting him to sit. In a moment of vulnerability, she gave him a somewhat PG-rated version of the story that hit Wrigley like an NC-17.

"I think it's Biggs," Wrigley blurted out.

"Think?" Annie said, raising an eyebrow.

"Ok, *know*," he said guiltily. "I caught him from my room, dropping off a box a few days ago. I didn't want to say anything because I, uh, love cannoli."

"Damn him," Annie said to herself. "Well, go over there and thank him. Then tell him to stop."

"Do I have to?" Wrigley asked.

"Wrigs, he's just trying to be your friend. You could use one, you know. His mom says he's a very good ballplayer."

Wrigley looked unsure, but he realized Annie was right. Later that day, he called Biggs on his cell phone. It was the first time Annie had actually seen Wrigley dial a phone, let alone call a friend. She was so giddy she had to leave the room.

"Santino's!" Regina said, answering the phone.

"I…ah…ah…this is Wrigley. Could I please talk to Biggs?"

"Sure, Wrigley, hold on," Regina said, over the roar in the background.

"Hello?" Biggs said. "Wrigley?"

"Hi, Biggs," Wrigley said, "Just wanted to say thanks for the cannoli. Mom says you can stop bringing them now."

"Hah," Biggs laughed. "Not stopping 'til we play catch."

Wrigley pondered for a moment, his stomach and head in disagreement.

"Mom says you're a player," Wrigley said.

"I can hold my own," Biggs said.

★ ★ ★

Wrigley answered the door himself, his ambi-glove on his right hand. And there was Biggs, his plain ol' regular glove on his left.

"Come on," said Wrigley, guiding Biggs through the house toward the sliding door in the back.

"That's a weird glove?" Biggs said.

"It's an ambi-glove—for pitching with both arms," Wrigley said.

Biggs just nodded his head. *Sure.* He was not really listening because he was floored upon seeing the full-sized mound Connor had built. The mound looked just like a professional one, with smooth, manicured edges between the grass and the dirt. The backstop was also pro-looking. The quality of the whole setup surprised Biggs. It truly looked like a major league mound and home plate. *This kid is serious about baseball*, Biggs thought. He turned to look at Wrigley, a huge smile on his face. "Okay," Biggs said, "that's one beautiful pitcher's mound."

"My grandpa made it," Wrigley said. "He used to work for the Cubs as a groundskeeper. He's dead now. My mom and I keep it up. She's my personal catcher."

"That's cool. Okay. Let's take this slow," Biggs waved the ball earnestly in front of Wrigley's face. "Can you, uh, see it?"

Wrigley waved his hands out searching for the ball, playacting like he was blind while Biggs stood dumbfounded, not sure how to react. Then, Wrigley changed character and grabbed the ball out of Biggs' hand in a flash. "I see it! I have a new set of eyes!"

"Okay, okay," said Biggs, laughing, "You had me there for a sec." He walked back about five feet, put the ball in his throwing hand, and seemed like he was ready to softly toss it to Wrigley.

"What are you doing?" Wrigley asked.

"Playing catch," Biggs said.

"I can play *real* catch!" Wrigley said, a little offended, and Biggs, not sure what he was dealing with backed up another 25 feet.

"Is *this* okay," Biggs said sarcastically.

"Fine. Let's warm up." Wrigley said. After they tossed the ball back and forth silently for about five minutes, Wrigley said, "I don't see like you do but I can pretty much track the ball, even see the seams if I concentrate."

"That's good. I just didn't know," Biggs said.

"Sorry I messed with you."

"No worries," said Biggs.

"I'm ready to pitch."

Biggs opened his hands inviting him to let 'er rip. Wrigley walked back to the mound and scratched at the rubber. Biggs squatted down in a catcher's position behind the plate, which was meticulously built by Connor, complete with dirt and batter's box. He squatted and pounded his mitt, inviting Wrigley to fire one in. Wrigley wound up, imitating Sandy Koufax to a tee and let go of a fastball. It zipped into Biggs' mitt with a loud pop before he could move it.

"*YeeeeeeOW!*" Biggs yelled, taking the glove off and shaking out his hand. "That was some heater!"

Annie heard the pop and the yell, and smiling—she had a feeling Wrigley didn't know his own strength—went to the hallway bin where they stored their baseball gloves, grabbed the orange extra-padded catcher's mitt and carried it out to the backyard.

"Yo, Biggs," Annie said as she tossed the catcher's mitt to him.

"Thanks, Mrs. Sanders. Wrigley has some heat."

"Yup," Annie smiled. "Please, call me Annie."

Wrigley had a huge smile on his face. But not just because of the satisfying pop and Biggs' response. He could *see* the spin of the ball's seams and where it hit the mitt. This was a whole lot easier. Wrigley threw about 20 pitches from the left side before switching his glove to the right.

"Wait, you were *serious* about both arms?" Biggs said.

"Sure. Papa taught me," Wrigley said.

"Unreal. Okay, bring it," Biggs said.

Wrigley threw about 10 more pitches, mostly Satchel Paige fastballs that seemed to pop the mitt even louder. Biggs had a hard time catching them, and his hand was stinging something awful, even with the catcher's mitt. Wrigley clearly wasn't done, but Biggs needed a pause. "How about a snack or something?" he asked.

Wrigley was confused; he was just getting warmed up. "Sure," he said, shrugging his shoulders. Then he smiled. "The cannoli man didn't come today, but Mom's got ice cream."

"You know, Wrigley," Biggs said, tossing the baseball in the air and catching it in his mitt as they walked into the house, "the gang is having a ball game tomorrow. You wanna come?"

Wrigley looked up at Biggs, a little suspicious. "Nah, thanks. I don't think…"

"It'll be fun," Biggs interrupted. "I promise."

Annie, in the kitchen washing dishes, overheard the boys. "Why not, Wrigs, why not? Don't you always daydream about pitching?" she couldn't help herself. "You'd get a chance to pitch to live hitters, like *real* baseball."

Wrigley shot his mom a look that said *mind your own business*, but inside, he quickly decided she was right—*live* hitters—and he did a backflip. "Okay, I'm game," he said as he walked over to the freezer.

CHAPTER 6

"Left one up," Wrigley said to Toothpick, shaking the cobwebs out after his third hit of smelling salts. "Won't do that again."

"I'll take it from here," Toothpick said to the trainer.

"Suit yourself," said the trainer and walked off the field.

"Now is your time, Wrigley," said Toothpick. "Get in your zone." Then he pointed to Wrigley's head and said, "Listen to Vinny. Let him help you. I didn't see you do any self-talk that last pitch. What were you thinking?"

Wrigley nodded his head in acquiescence. His head hurt but not too bad. "Guess I was nervous. Everything moved too fast."

"Remember to breathe," Toothpick calmly said. "It's time for you to deliver. Do your thing."

"Okay, okay, but first I gotta ask you something," Wrigley said. "Did your dad talk about how it felt to pitch with the bases loaded and a no-hitter on the line?"

"Yes," Toothpick lied. "He said it was the most fun he'd ever had in his life." In truth, his dad had refused to talk about it, saying he'd lived that moment once and didn't need to again. "Just have fun, Wrigs."

"Okay," Wrigley said as Toothpick put the ball in his glove. "I got this. I'll breathe…have fun."

★ ★ ★

The Lasaine Gang was a motley crew of mischief-makers bound by a love of baseball. When they weren't on the ball field or in detention, they peed in gas tanks, broke windows with footballs, and catcalled sunbathers. That Wrigley might join their ranks made Annie uncomfortably delighted.

"Hey, Wrigs," Annie said to Wrigley in his room getting dressed for the game. "Be your best out there. Remember to breathe. Let me show you a good one."

Annie took in a big breath and let it out slowly with a soft "ummmmm."

Wrigley took in a big breath, and let it out slowly, with a soft "paa paa," then smiled at his mom, who nodded. Then he pointed up to the sky.

"Okay, that'll work," Annie said, smiling. "Use that if you're hitting—or if you get on the mound. It'll help you relax. When you're throwing, just pretend you're in the den watching film. Be your favorite pitcher and have fun. Okay?"

"Sure, Mom. What do you think, Overall or Koufax?"

"That's your call, kid," Annie said.

"I think Koufax. I don't have control of my drop ball yet."

The doorbell rang. Biggs stood outside wearing a pair of cutoff jeans and a white t-shirt, carrying his glove underneath his right arm.

"Is the fireballer ready?" Biggs asked.

"Oh, he was *born* ready," Annie joked. "Come on in. Let me see how he's doing."

Annie walked to Wrigley's room and found him putting a batting glove in his back pocket—his *pièce de résistance*. He stood proud in front of the mirror in full Cubs uniform, complete with baseball shoes and a grey and pinstriped black 1908 World Series road hat worn by the World Champion Cubbies.

"What do you think?" Wrigley asked, crossing his arms and posing for his mom.

"You look like a ballplayer," Annie said. "Like a closer. Just have fun and throw!"

"Thanks, Mom," Wrigley said, smiling. As nonchalant as he was the day before, now he was like a shaken soda ready to burst, the black curls messily poking out from his cap like suds.

Wrigley marched out to the living room, and Annie following him proudly.

"Whoa!" Biggs said. "*Now* you're talking Cubs baseball."

Wrigley smiled his big, toothy smile, turned to wave goodbye, and his glasses fell off. He frantically searched for them but couldn't find them, even though they were just a few feet away.

Biggs picked them up and meticulously placed them on his face. "There you go—now you look like Rick 'Wild Thing' Vaughn."

"Who?" Wrigley replied, adjusting his glasses so that they were crooked.

"Never mind," said Biggs. "See ya, Mrs. San…Annie!"

"Have fun, boys!" she said, closing the door behind them, then, placing her back against the door, she slid to the floor.

★ ★ ★

At the field, Biggs lined up most of the gang and introduced them to Wrigley one at a time. The boys were reluctant to take orders, but Biggs, clearly the alpha, had control over them.

Wrigley, for his part, was wide-eyed, trying to soak in the baseball field. This was the first time he'd actually seen this park with his new eyes. He noticed the backstop made out of green wood and chain link fencing – crisp and clear. He stared over toward each dugout—cement bunkers that had roofs to shield the players from the elements. *What a field*, thought Wrigley. *This is baseball!*

"Wrigley, Wrigley?" Biggs said, trying to get his attention. But Wrigley didn't hear him, even though his big saddle bag hearing aids were all strapped on and working. Wrigley was completely distracted by actually seeing the details of the ballpark for the first time. Finally, Biggs came up to Wrigley and tapped him on the arm.

"Wrigley, meet Monty Jack," Biggs said, pointing to the smallest of the kids, a skinny boy about eight with a shaved head and red high-top tennis shoes. "*Manners*, Monty…"

Monty stuck out his hand toward Wrigley like a petulant child, "What's with the Cubs uni?"

Wrigley shook Monty's hand and smiled, revealing his sharp-edged crooked teeth to the crew. "I'm a Cubs fan. But my favorite pitcher is Koufax."

"Cool," said Monty Jack. "Man those are some teeth! Vampire?"

"Monty!" Biggs said, staring Monty Jack down. Then Biggs turned to George, a strongly built fourteen-year-old dressed in overalls, sporting an Alice Cooper t-shirt, who offered Wrigley a friendly, "Hey. I'm George."

"Hi," Wrigley said back.

Wrigley met Black Patty with his big, wild orange-red afro; Work, named so because, in addition to school, he had four jobs but managed to hang out with the guys and get some cuts in between shifts; Mary Jane Smith, a tomboy who was a dead ringer for Tatum O'Neal's Amanda Whurlitzer in *The Bad News Bears*; Dice, a slick, well-dressed import from New York City; Bobby V., a stocky Hispanic boy built like a brick shithouse; and Bobby F., a tall, lean American Indian wearing a Washington Redskins jersey. Wrigley was clearly confused by this one, his eyes darting from his face to his jersey to his face to his jersey.

Bobby F. got the reaction he wanted and smiled. "Nice to meecha, rookie."

"Elliott should be here in a bit," said Biggs.

"Does *everyone* have a nickname?" Wrigley whispered to Biggs.

"Yup," Biggs said. "Do you have one?"

"My grandpa started calling me Sandy, for Sandy Koufax."

"Sandy. I like that." Biggs said.

"Yeah, that's cool," said Monty Jack, and with that, removed the chip on his shoulder.

A boom box, blasting loud music, could be heard before it was seen. Out from the alley strutted Elliott Mason, a tall blond with a bowl haircut, blue eyes, and a cigarette sticking out of his mouth. Everyone turned to Elliott, then back to Biggs. Elliott came walking up with a cocky jaunt and took in Mr. Cubbie with the thick-framed glasses. "Who invited freako?"

The fellas' stifled laughter was worse than if they had just been hysterical. Biggs gave them a punishing look.

"Let's just pick," Biggs said. It was clear that this Elliott character was Biggs' foil.

"I got *him*…" Biggs said with a wry grin. "Sandy, come on over here."

Wrigley walked over and stood by Biggs, biting his lip, struggling to hold back a grin. He was thankful he had not been passed over. He was picked. Heck, he was picked first. Elliott shook his head derisively and picked George. They went through the gang until everyone had a team. Most games went a full nine innings, and this game was no exception. Wrigley played right field most of the game and did not get a single ball hit to him. But he was ready to go. He figured if it came his way, he'd let it bounce, then track it down and throw the guy out at second. He had worse luck at the plate. He had struck out every at bat, with Elliott pitching, and pitching hard. One time, Elliott threw high heat near Wrigley's chin and Biggs yelled at him to "cut it out." But still, he was having the time of his life playing real baseball with a bunch of kids.

Life couldn't be too much better than this. Now, in the bottom of the 9th, it was tied five to five, with two men on base, and Elliott at the plate. Biggs' pitcher Black Patty had walked the last two batters.

"Sandy!" Biggs waved to Wrigley in right field, "Come on in!"

Biggs assumed correctly that Wrigley didn't hear him, so he waved him in with both arms. Wrigley saw Biggs, pointed to his own chest questioningly. "Me?" he mouthed.

"Yeah, Sandy, this is the call to the bullpen!"

"Huh?" Wrigley said. He just couldn't hear him very well, but he knew what he wanted. The gang started laughing a little and then Elliott yelled out to Wrigley. "Hey, retard, he wants you to pitch."

Wrigley, barely hearing Elliott but reading his lips, now embarrassed suddenly lost his nerve. "That's okay!" he yelled back, "I'm fine out here!"

Biggs ran out to Wrigley in a hurry. "We need you, Wrigs. Black Patty's done. Come on, you can do this."

They both trotted in from right field for a moment. Then Wrigley stopped, mesmerized by the infield dirt, while Biggs kept going without realizing Wrigley had stopped.

"Oh, come on," said Elliott. "You're not letting that retard pitch to me. He's staring at the dirt! I want to win this game fair and square. He's gonna walk me and Monty Jack. Game over."

"What?" said Biggs sauntering up to him, "you afraid of a little…*challenge?*"

Elliott scoffed, then kicked at the dirt around the plate and said, "Bring him on."

Biggs turned to see Wrigley was still in the infield, now with a handful of dirt, analyzing the particles. Biggs lost his patience and yelled out, "Wrigley, let's go!"

Hearing Biggs say "Wrigley" instead of "Sandy" or "Wrigs," he felt like he did when his mom called him "Wrigley B. Sanders" when she wasn't playing around anymore. The "B" stood for "Bert." Wrigley bolted right in.

At the mound, Wrigley looked up at Biggs with a nervous smile, "This feels a little…different."

"You'll be fine. This isn't Dodger Stadium. Do you need to loosen up a bit?" Biggs asked.

"Just a couple," Wrigley said.

"Pitch the way you pitched in your backyard," whispered Biggs, "and this meathead's a goner."

Wrigley threw a couple of easy strikes to Work, who sat behind the plate, and nodded that he was ready. He'd never had a batter in the batter's box before, and Elliott was giving him a glare, like he was going to deliberately hit a line-drive right back at him. Wrigley waddled to the back of the mound, took a deep breath, and in his mind, transformed himself—the diminutive, bespectacled, white ducky—into the very image of the 6'2" lefty Sandy Koufax.

"Help me, Papa," he whispered to himself, taking a peek up to heaven. He took one big breath, letting out a low "paa paa" on the exhale then looked in for the sign.

"What are you doing?" screamed Work. "We don't give *signs*…"

Ignoring him, Wrigley nodded his head "yes" and decided to do a modification of Satchel Paige's windup, but left handed because he wanted to pitch lefty like Sandy. He wound his arm clockwise twice, rocked back, brought both his hands behind his head, where he held them for a long pause, then straight up above his head for a moment, then, in a gangly, old-fashioned move that none of these kids except Biggs had ever seen—because Biggs had seen Satchel Paige on film—started his glide toward home plate, letting go of a Sandy K style rising fastball that may have topped 60 miles per hour.

"Yeeeeee-OW!" screamed Work. He didn't even see the ball, he just felt it hit where he held his glove.

"Striiiike!" yelled Biggs from his position at first base.

Elliott backed out of the box. "Lucky pitch, four eyes," he said to Wrigley. "I bet you can't even *see* the glove. Do that again and I'll put it into Mr. Henderson's yard."

Wrigley whispered Annie's words to himself, using her intonation "Just have fun and throw," then reared back, quick-pitching a Chet Hoff old-timer "roundhouse" curve—a very slow-moving ball that looked like it was three feet off the plate, then slowly, ever so slowly, curved and hit Elliott right on the shoulder. It was half as fast as the first pitch, barely fast enough to break tissue paper, but Elliott dropped his bat, glared at Wrigley and said, "You wanna have some fun, retard?"

"Oh shit," said Biggs, looking right at Elliott. "He didn't do that on purpose!" Biggs screamed, but he knew it was on.

Elliott was running with full intent toward the mound, ready to pound Wrigley into oblivion, and as he prepared to unleash a big haymaker, Biggs dive-tackled him a yard from the rubber. Everyone darted from their positions to join the fray. Wrigley, stepping back from the mound, didn't know quite what to do. He just stood on the back of the mound, in full Cubs regalia, trying to blend in with his surroundings, hoping they wouldn't hurt him. Wrigley just sort of glanced down at the pack that seemed to be smiling as they clawed and poked and grappled at each other. Biggs and Elliott looked dead serious, though.

There was clearly some bad blood between these guys. Out of breath, once the smoke cleared, Work held each boy at bay, palm in chests.

"Okay?" he said, looking at Biggs. "Okay!" he said more forcefully, glaring at Elliott.

"Whatever!" said Elliott, swatting Work's arm off of him. And turning to Wrigley, he yelled, "You're *dead,* retard!"

The Lasaine Gang settled back in to their positions. "Bottom of the 9th," said Biggs, smacking a fist in to his glove. "One out. Tie ball game. Bases loaded…"

"Play ball!" called Work. Wrigley looked in to the catcher, again waiting for a sign. Work rolled his eyes and dropped his middle finger. Wrigley looked confused, but nodded, and then slowly went into his left-handed windup. He put his hands behind his head, reached back, and at the last second decided to use Fernando's windup. He looked up to the sky for a good long pause—just like Fernando Valenzuela. As he paused, he heard a quick footstep then felt a sudden pain near his chin. Everything went black, and he had the sensation of falling to the ground in slow motion, which he did. He heard the peculiar sound of his new glasses getting stepped on and then the noise of another Lasaine Gang riot. Both sides were brawling, kind of aimlessly, looking like children in a friendly pillow fight. Wrigley tried to get up, but got gently pushed back down a few times by Biggs who whispered, "Stay down."

"You dirty son of a bitch," Biggs screamed at Elliott, grabbing him in a headlock. You cold cocked him in the middle of a pitch. Who does that?"

Biggs had a tight grip on him. "You're…choking…me," Biggs heard him gurgle and finally dropped him. Elliott began desperately trying to get air back in his lungs.

"Asshole!" Elliott said but recoiled as Biggs gestured to take another crack at him.

Everybody dusted off their clothes, with some slowly walking off the field with Elliott, making sure he was ok, with him angrily shrugging off the sympathetic gestures. "I'm fine!"

Biggs yelled to Elliott as he limped away. "You're out. Game over. We win."

"Whatever…" he responded under his breath, then stopped and glared at Wrigley. "Next time I pound *you*, retard!"

"Huh? Wrigley said, acting like he didn't quite hear Elliot.

Wrigley felt a lump under his right eye. His glasses were crushed in the dust, with one arm of his new glasses broken off and one piece of glass demolished.

"You okay?" Biggs softly asked after everyone had cleared the area.

"Yeah," Wrigley said, dazed. "Did we win?"

★ ★ ★

Biggs dropped Wrigley off at the door, complete with puffy eye and broken glasses in hand.

"Sorry, Annie," Biggs said, embarrassedly. "I tried to protect him."

Annie took a look at Wrigley, and once she noticed he was more embarrassed than hurt, she felt a slight burst of *joy*. "Thanks, Biggs. See you soon?" she said hopefully.

Biggs, feeling guilty, looked at her confused. She seemed earnest. "Sure?" Biggs responded.

Annie smiled. "Say hi to your mom."

She guided Wrigley into the bathroom and started wiping blood off his cheek. That's when she noticed a smile on his face. "What happened?" she asked.

"We played a ball game," Wrigley said.

"And?" Annie asked, kind of gleeful.

"It ended in a fight, but we won," Wrigley said cracking an even bigger smile.

Annie's face went white. She didn't like the word "*fight*."

"It's okay, Mom," Wrigley said, comforting her. "Really. I got to pitch to a real hitter." Then he looked in the mirror and assessed damage, shaking his head and chuckling at the Quasimodo staring back. "Crazy Elliott."

Annie paused, realizing that Wrigley might be crazier than she was. *What would Dad do in this situation?* she thought. A part of her was proud of Wrigley for getting his hands dirty with other kids and emerging maybe *better* for the wear. A part of her was itching to call Regina, track down this Elliott character and return the favor.

"Okay, Wrigs," she said, affecting an understanding tone, but betraying skepticism, "tell me about it."

"I'm the new kid, Mom. A lot of them were nice. A couple, not so much. Biggs brought me in to pitch in the bottom of the 9th, and I threw a strike to Elliott."

"Wow," said Annie. "First-pitch strike…*nice*. What'd ya use?"

"Started him off with a Satchel Paige heater thrown lefty, then went to a Chet Hoff roundhouse curve—the same one he used to strike out Ty Cobb, except mine hit Elliott in the shoulder."

"And what did Crazy Elliott do then?" Annie asked.

"Well, in the middle of my Valenzuela windup, he cold cocked me and…"

"Wait, *what*?" Annie said, cutting him off. "You got him back, right? Did you at least bean him with a heater?"

"No," Wrigley said, looking down to the ground. "During the fight, Biggs kept telling me to stay down, so I did."

Annie looked unsure. She was hoping the tale finished with a *you should see the other guy*.

"But it was awesome," Wrigley said. "I got to pitch to a real live hitter. And we won. I get to do that, I don't care what they do to me."

Annie looked at Wrigley's bloody face. He was no longer the little boy who *dreamed of pitching*. He was a young man *pitching*. She winked at him and said, "Guess you're okay and that's all that matters. What ya say we head on over to Cavaretta's for some cannoli to celebrate your first save?"

"First save," Wrigley said to himself, then, breaking into his biggest smile yet, "Cool!"

Annie reached over to the sink drawer and pulled out the spare pair of glasses for Wrigley. She kept them for just such an occasion—in case his first pair broke roughhousing with *friends*. She put the glasses on his face. Wrigley adjusted them, making them just a little crooked, and looked in the mirror. "Perfect," he said. "Thanks Mom. Oh, and Mom, these glasses are really cool. I'm really seeing great, but I think I need some new hearing aids. I, uh, I couldn't hear so great today."

"Oh my goodness! Yes, Wrigley, yes," Annie said, feeling terrible that she just hadn't thought of upgrading his hearing aids.

CHAPTER 7

"Boys, what'll it be?" asked the MLB umpire, motioning that it was time to pitch.

"We're good," Toothpick said and trotted off the field, thinking Wrigley was going to need his best stuff to get out of this jam.

"Oh my, looks like Wrigley Sanders is up for the task," Vinny said. "Here we are in the top of the 13th, bases loaded, no outs, and the Cubbies are down by a run and up comes the Yankees' number-two hitter, Derek Jeter." Wrigley's knees didn't feel like they were about to buckle anymore, and his head wasn't spinning as much.

He took off his cap, wiped the sweat off his head, walked to the back of the mound, took a big, deep breath, let out a low "paa paa," pointed to the sky, then came back toward the rubber, and put his cap on tight, ready to pitch. That's when Wrigley looked to the stands and saw him—Orval Overall. All six feet two inches of him, standing right behind the Cubs' dugout, dressed in 1908 pinstripes. He looked just like the poster Wrigley used to have in his room when he was a kid, except he was alive. Well, kind of, because it seemed to Wrigley that most of the other people were in full color but Overall was in ghostly shades of grey.

★ ★ ★

The Santino's 1960s ranch-style house was one of thousands of tract homes, most with a two-car garage and good-sized yards front and back. A number of kids hung out on the Santino curb. Wrigley arrived armed with his new hearing aids, which really helped, and knocked on the front door. It seemed really, really loud! Biggs opened the door, and as they went inside, they turned a corner to the right and found Bubbs in the den, sitting on a small wooden rocking chair with a faded Cubs shawl over her skinny, frail body, watching the Cubs game on TV.

"Oh come on Gracie, you can do it!" Bubbs said as she rubbed her crooked grey fingers over the baseball card of the Cubbies' first baseman. The big lefty was at the plate, with a three, two count. He slapped a double down the right field line.

"Yeah! Thatta boy!" she yelled, raising her bony mottled arms high in the air as the ball rolled down right field line. "Stand up! Stand up!" Mark Grace confidently strode in to second with a double.

"Bubbs," Biggs said. She didn't respond. "Bubbs?" he inquired, a little more forcefully.

She picked another card out of her quiver of baseball cards and started rubbing on it.

"*Grandma!*" Biggs finally yelled. Bubbs slowly turned to Biggs, looked him right in the eye and said, "I'm busy here, Biggs. Come back some other time."

Wrigley enjoyed actually hearing all of their conversation. But he was also taking in the cool Cubs memorabilia on the walls. He stared at a photo of Ron Santo at the Mets' Shea Stadium in 1969 in the on-deck circle where a black cat crossed his path. Wrigley knew the story. The Cubbies had a 9½ game lead over the Mets late in the season and were a shoo-in for the playoffs. But seemingly from that moment on, they went on an epic losing streak, blowing their lead—one of the biggest collapses in baseball history. Wrigley moved on to a framed yet faded-yellow article about Billy Cianis and his goat Murphy getting kicked out of Wrigley during the 1945 World Series. Next to that was a picture of Billy wearing a suit and a hat, at the gate with his goat, an usher asking him to leave—because his goat stank. Wrigley knew the legend well. Allegedly, Billy had said, "The Cubs ain't gonna win no more. The Cubs will never win a World Series as long as my goat is not allowed in Wrigley Field." From that day forward, the Cubs went on the longest running streak of bad luck for any team in the history of the sport, referred to as "The Curse of the Billy Goat." Next to this photo was a telegram from Billy Cianis that read, "Who *stinks* now?" addressed to P. K. Wrigley, the owner of the Cubs who made the decision to kick Cianis and his goat out of Wrigley Field. *Is that telegram real?* Wrigley wondered, leaning in.

"Wrigs!" Biggs called out, startling him. "I want you to meet Bubbs."

Wrigley bee lined over to the rocking chair. Bubbs was still immersed in the game. Wrigley squinted at the TV. Sammy Sosa was coming toward the batter's box after talking to the third-base coach. He jumped over the baseline but brushed the chalk with his cleats.

"What! $#!@. *No!*" Bubbs yelled. "You don't touch the third baseline!" As if suffering a spell of fatigue, she sunk back in to her chair, feeling defeated. "Inning *over*."

Biggs smiled at Wrigley, then shrugged, fascinated by Bubbs.

"You wanna catch some of this?" she asked, gruffly.

"Ye…yeah, sh…sure," Wrigley responded, as if he had a choice. He settled down on the couch. Biggs joined him, amused at Wrigley's response. On the first pitch, Sosa popped out to the pitcher, inning over.

"You know better than to distract me during a game," Bubbs glared at Biggs. Then she looked straight at Wrigley and scrutinized him with what he imagined were eyes that were as bad as his—or at least as bad as his once were.

"Who is this?" she snapped. She then noticed his 1908 Cubs hat, and correctly assessing what it was, nodded toward it. "Nice old-timer Cubbie hat. What's your name, kid?" she asked.

"Wrigley," he responded, a frog caught in his throat.

"What was that?" Bubbs asked, thrusting her left ear in his direction.

"Wrigley!" he spoke up. Then softening a bit, "But some call me Sandy, ma'am. Like Sandy Koufax."

"I'll stick with Wrigley. And so should you." Bubbs smiled with three crooked, barely-hanging-on teeth showing between her grey wrinkly lips.

"My grandpa worked for Mr. Wrigley himself," Wrigley bragged.

Bubbs cocked her head at Wrigley, "You *Connor's* grandkid?"

"Ye…yes, ma'am."

"Hope you got the guy who gave you that shiner," said Bubbs. Wrigley looked up at Biggs, not sure how to respond.

"You wanna help out?" Bubbs asked, changing the subject. "I've been working hard all day here trying to break this Philly spell. You know about jinxes, son?" Wrigley looked over to Biggs, who just grinned.

"We need to break them damn spells or we're never going to win a World Series. We gotta stop all of them. The Philly spell, the Billy Goat jinx, the black cat, Bartman! Do you believe that? How did *that* happen?"

Bubbs was getting animated now, and Biggs knew that she could go on for some time. She didn't seem to bother Wrigley. In fact, he leaned forward, seemingly interested in Bubbs' semi-hysterical banter.

"I'm gonna get some chips," Biggs said. "You want something to drink, Wrigs?"

"I'm good," Wrigley said.

"You believe in voodoo?" Bubbs asked as Biggs disappeared into the kitchen. She reached into the drawer of the side table that sat to the right of the rocking chair and pulled out a handful of crude dolls in baseball uniforms.

"These are opposing pitchers," she said holding the bunch ominously by the necks. Wrigley noticed they had rough-hewn faces and hair that matched each pitcher's features: one looked like Philly pitcher Mike Mimbs, another like Paul Quantrill.

"She twists their arms, slams them to the ground, spits on them, just about everything but put needles in them," Biggs said returning to the den with a bag of chips. "You don't do *that*, do you, Bubbs?" Biggs laughed. Bubbs shot him a dirty look.

"And what happens?" Wrigley asked.

"Sit down, Wrigley," she said, but he was already sitting down.

Biggs knew this was going to take at least an hour or two, so he interrupted his grandma. "Wrigs, I have to set up for a jam. Band's due here in less than 10. You okay here?"

"Yeah, I'll be fine," Wrigley said. Bubbs was handing him the dolls one by one, and Wrigley was fascinated and somehow disturbed by the cotton oozing from the loose seams.

Bubbs found the doll of the Phillies pitcher Curt Shilling, who was on the mound. "When I twist a man's arm," Bubbs said, torqueing the doll's right arm with disturbing rigor, "he falls apart." With that, Bubbs gave the right arm one more twist and set the doll down on top of her TV tray. She looked at him and smiled, suddenly seeming like the witch in Disney's *Snow White*. Like Snow White, Wrigley was enticed.

"Ball four," they heard from the TV. One walk was followed by another walk and a bloop single. With each turn of events, Bubbs' eyes grew brighter, and she sat just a little straighter in her chair.

"Cubs win, Cubs win," Bubbs muttered under her breath as she stared at the TV screen, and then gave the doll a twist at the torso. And sure enough, a fly ball, with a little more zip than Wrigley had seen all season long, was launched over the centerfield fence for a grand slam.

"Amazing!" Wrigley said, turning to Bubbs but she looked like she had fallen asleep. *Or maybe that she was de…*

"Not dead yet, kiddo!" Bubbs suddenly yelled.

Wrigley, who had leaned in to see what was up, flew backwards, his butt hitting the end of the couch, and plopping down on the floor.

He popped back up, and sat on the couch, trying to re-stick the bad landing. He removed his glasses and wiped off Bubbs' spittle with his shirt. Bubbs gave him a sly smile, amused by her ability to mess with him.

"I was born in 1908, on October 14, the same day the Cubs won the World Series," Bubbs said. She went on to tell him about the 1908 team like they were living, breathing friends of hers, including Three-Fingered Mordecai Brown, the famous double-play combination of Tinkers and Evers to Chance. She said she talked to Frank Chance, who played and managed for the Cubs, on a regular basis.

"You were friends with Frank Chance?" Wrigley asked.

"Well," she said, tilting her hand back and forth. She opened the side-table drawer one more time and took out a badly worn Chance baseball card and held it to her heart. "Sort of…"

"Holy crap!" said Wrigley, unable to contain himself. "That's a T206 Frank Chance!" Wrigley knew that in mint condition it was worth over $25,000. This one was anything but mint. *But still, a T206 Frank Chance! Cool!*

Bubbs smiled, "How about you, Wrigley? You play ball?"

"Yes," Wrigley said proudly. "I'm a pitcher. A *closer*"

Bubbs cracked a smile. "That grandpa of yours," she said. "He had the talent to make it as a pitching coach in the majors. Did you know that?" Then her face turned dark and she squinted her eyes. "That blond she-devil jinxed him," she said. "He used to play in pick-up games with the likes of Joe DiMaggio and was the *real* coach of some of the Cubby greats—Claude Passeau and Dizzy Dean…"

Wrigley stared wide-eyed.

"Mm-hmm," said Bubbs. "All the stars were lined up for Connor, but it all went south when he met that white-haired vixen."

She shivered and then looked back at Wrigley, sitting there, waiting for Bubbs to continue. "I like you, Wrigley," she said. "You can come watch the Cubs with me any time."

"I'll do that," Wrigley said smiling. He stood up and stuck out his hand. Bubbs took his hand and gave it the firmest handshake he'd ever gotten. He felt sorry for the dolls.

"See you around, Bubbs."

CHAPTER 8

Wrigley looked around and saw more ghostly old-timer pitchers in the grandstands, all dressed in 1908 garb. One at a time, they started to stand, including Sam "Toothpick" Jones, Toothpick's daddy. Sam looked a lot like Toothpick, actually, the other way around. He looked back at the rest of the old-timers and saw them all smacking balls in their mitts, in full uniform, staring at Wrigley. Something told Wrigley they all wanted to pitch, all ached to get in on the action. But one at a time, they all slowly sat back down, nodding, smiling or waving at Wrigley. All except Orval Overall, who looked right at Wrigley and said, "Drop ball." Somehow Wrigley heard him. Wrigley shook his head and looked away, trying to clear his mind, but when he looked back, Orval was still there. In fact, he winked at Wrigley and nodded. Wrigley turned back to home and glanced in for a sign. He saw an orange-colored mitt with a younger, more vibrant version of Papa Connor behind the plate. Wrigley froze!

"It's okay," Connor said, "It's baseball. Anything can happen. Just trust your stuff."

"What the hell?" Wrigley said. His brain was spinning out. *First Orval Overall on the mound, now Papa behind the plate. What the…and now, who is that?*

Wrigley watched as up to the plate strolled the living, breathing embodiment of confidence—the Yankees' Mike Donlin. Connor had told his story to Wrigley once. Donlin was a well-known professional actor who played baseball back in 1908. Wrigley had seen his baseball card. He'd hit 334, a better average than Ty Cobb had that year. Donlin would not be an easy out.

"Well," Vin Scully drawled, "Wrigley Sanders looks a little confused on the mound right now. His head is literally spinning left to right, the result of a pretty nasty hit to the head, I imagine. But Derek Jeter isn't going to wait all day for a pitch. Oh, here we go! Finally, Wrigley is toeing the rubber…"

★ ★ ★

Mr. English's five-acre property called "The Farm" with its huge eucalyptus trees surrounding the perimeter, was home to hundreds of big, black, noisy crows as well as Mr. English and his chickens, who supplied the local markets with farm-fresh eggs. A warm Santa Ana breeze blew through the trees, rustling in the early morning light. The farm was the site of many an army battle plus riding bikes over jumps, and of course, egg fights—tons of unsanctioned egg fights. On this Sunday, everyone from the block stood in silence as 12-inch wooden stakes with little red flags flapped in the breeze. They surrounded the farm, diced up into neat little squares that staked out a future housing subdivision.

"Those assholes are going to ruin our farm," Elliott said, breaking the silence. "Hoffstetter is building tract homes."

"I think you're right," said Biggs, reluctant to agree with Elliott.

"He is," George said. "My dad told me."

Wrigley, looking up at Biggs and Elliott, slowly walked over to a stake and pulled it out. Elliott, Biggs, George, and the rest of the gang glanced around at each other, shrugged, and followed suit, pulling the rest of the stakes out of the ground. Cautiously, at first, then with more resolve—even a little glee.

"Not gonna let it happen," said Biggs, yanking the stakes out and derisively casting them aside.

"No way," said George.

"Ow!" said Wrigley, holding his left hand.

"What?" said Elliott annoyed, taking pause from his own vandalism.

Wrigley held up a finger. "Splinter," he said, forcing a smile, feeling embarrassed by his outburst. A police car pulled up about 50 yards away on the street.

"Crap, crap, CRAP!" said Elliott. "Make a run for it!"

"Hold up!" one of the officers yelled, breaking after them.

This made everyone run just a little faster, and they would've outrun the fuzz had Wrigley, not knowing the terrain, seen the huge hole in the ground. Everyone else ran around the jump that had been built up over the years for bicycles. Wrigley ran right into the gap, flipped end over end and landed face down. Biggs and George took one look at Wrigley, saw how close the police were and decided they had better keep running. Wrigley rolled over slowly, dazed, and found his glasses. Realizing they had survived the crash, he smiled to himself, cleaned them once with his shirt, put them on, and looked up to see the two officers.

"How…howdy," Wrigley said, giving them a slight nervous wave, knowing he was in trouble.

"What you boys doing?" one of the officers said, hands on his hips.

"Playing army?" Wrigley replied.

"I don't think Mr. Hoffstetter would appreciate you boys taking out his stakes. Do you?"

"No," Wrigley said, looking down at the ground.

"Get on up, son," the other officer said, and held out his hand for Wrigley to grab. "Where do you live?"

"Around the corner," Wrigley said, defeated. None of the other guys had stuck around.

The officers looked at each other. "We're gonna take you home and have a chat with your parents." Wrigley nodded his head and imagined what sort of trouble he'd be in for. The officers flanked Wrigley, guiding him toward his house.

"That's the one," Wrigley said, weakly pointing, trying to procrastinate. The officers led him to the door and one rang the doorbell. No answer. He rang again. Nothing. Wrigley remembered that Annie was out shopping. He breathed a sigh of relief, then glanced up at the officer to his right, who was looking at his partner. He shrugged, and then looked down at Wrigley.

"We're going to let you off the hook today," said the older officer.

"But we don't want to catch you on that property again," chimed in the younger.

"Okay, okay," said Wrigley, putting up a Scout sign. "Thank you…sirs."

The officers left Wrigley sitting on his doorstep, head in hands. *Why did the gang leave me?* he thought. He felt a hand tapping his shoulder.

"Hey Wrigs," said Biggs. Wrigley looked up to see Biggs, Work, and George. "How you doin'?" Before he could say anything, Biggs launched into an apology. "We're sorry."

"*Real* sorry," chimed in Work.

"Promise we'll never do that again," said Biggs. George just looked downward, remorseful.

"What d'ya say?" said George, holding out his hand. Wrigley smiled and took it.

★ ★ ★

The next night, Wrigley stood in the middle of the block with his hands over his eyes. "Three, two, one…ready or not, here I come!" he yelled. He stood in the middle of the street, not a soul in sight. He ran from tree to tree, dropped to look under cars parked in driveways, checked behind shrubbery. Nothing. Was this a joke? Had they ditched him again? His exasperation was interrupted when he caught sight of a motorcycle parked at the curb. The rims glistened, beckoning him over. He walked around it reverently, and then ran his fingers alongside it.

"Harley Davidson," he said to himself. He scrutinized the hog and then looked around suddenly glad he was ditched.

Wrigley climbed on. He got in to a crouching position and made motor noises, starting with a rumble and accelerating into a roar. He could feel his thighs taut, a breeze through his hair, and a hand on his shoulder. The next thing he knew, Wrigley was on his back, straddled by, from this bottom angle, a giant. Clad in black leathers with impossibly thick muttonchops, the giant got in his face. His breath smelled of something like gasoline.

"I'm not looking for trouble!" Wrigley said, open hands in front of his face.

"Well you *found* it, turd," responded the biker.

Wrigley instinctively thrust a palm in to the biker's nose. Surprised by the power of the impact, the biker stumbled backward, cupping his hands over his face.

"My nose!" he screamed. "Broke my nose!" Wrigley jumped up and made a run for it, duck waddling down the asphalt road. The biker gathered himself and ran after Wrigley.

"You're dead meat!" he growled, easily catching up with Wrigley, grabbing him by the collar of his shirt, and turning him around. Wrigley saw the blood around the angry giant's mouth, and the sight terrified him. The giant reared his arm back like he was going toss a bowling ball and hit him twice in the gut. Wrigley doubled over with a grunt and dropped to the ground, gasping for air. The giant looked down at Wrigley, "You messed with the wrong dude, duck face," he said, wiping his nose with the back of his hand.

Wrigley got his wind back. "Duck face?" he mustered, gasping. "What does that even mea…" And with that, the giant kicked him in the ribs.

"I think he's had enough," Elliott said coming out from behind some hedges.

"You want some of this?" the biker responded. One by one, out came Biggs, George, Dice, Monty Jack, Mary Jane Smith, Black Patty, and the Bobbies. They surrounded the biker.

"The dude sucker-punched me," the biker said, suddenly defensive.

"You had it coming," Elliott said.

The biker made for Elliott, head down, like a charging bull. *Perfect*, thought Elliott, who shifted to his left and grabbed the biker in a headlock—the very same one Biggs had used on him during the baseball scuffle.

"Picked on the wrong crew, leather face," said Elliott, in complete control of the biker's body. Struggling just made the choke more severe, so he gave up and let Elliott lead him around like a miniature poodle on a choke chain. Elliott walked him over toward a large fifteen-foot-high sawgrass bush with huge, white, fluffy flowers and long, razor-sharp fronds.

The rest of the gang followed, a few of them already wincing, because this was one of Elliott's favorite types of torture.

"Let's have some fun," Elliott said.

"Pants him, Mary Jane!" said Monty Jack. Mary Jane broke out into a big smile, ran up behind the biker and yanked his leather pants, which were already riding a little low, down to his ankles.

The gang laughing, Elliott swung the biker's body like a dead squirrel in the mouth of a pit bull back and forth through the razor-sharp leaves of the sawgrass bush, the thin leaves ripping tiny cuts into his thighs and calves. The blood slowly started to ooze out of his legs, covering his legs with a red, shiny sheen.

"That's enough, Elliott," said Wrigley.

"Who asked *you*, retard?" Elliott said.

"He's right, Elliott. Let him go." Biggs said.

"I give, dude!" said the biker.

Elliott shrugged and pulled the biker out of the bush, staying ready if he was stupid enough to strike. The biker stood up, his head hidden beneath his leather jacket, which had been pulled over his head, leaving him looking like the headless, pantless horseman. The gang could hear him whimpering as he poked the top of his head from out of his jacket. Embarrassed, scared, and pants around his ankles, he stumbled back to his bike, where he quickly yanked up his drawers, straightened his jacket and got on his bike and started the engine. He revved it a few times, and took off. Elliott stuck up both middle fingers. When the last sputter of the bike faded away, the gang reveled in their success, high-fiving each other. All but Elliott, who stared off in the direction of the biker, fire still in his eyes.

"That sucker won't be messing with us again!" said George.

"No chance," said Monty Jack.

"Ain't never coming back," added Dice.

Wrigley went over to Elliott and held up his hand for a high-five, "Thanks, buddy."

"Save it, retard," Elliott said, slapping his waiting hand away.

CHAPTER 9

Donlin stepped into the batter's box with the confidence of a hitter at his peak. Wrigley took a quick glance over toward the pitcher's gallery. Everyone was sitting down except Orval Overall, who nodded at Wrigley and patted his mitt.

Wrigley backed off the mound, duck-walked around, announced to himself in a strange old-timer announcer's voice that he'd never used before: "This season Orval Overall has thrown a total of nine shut outs. No surprise with his most powerful pitch being his drop ball that actually disappears into thin air."

"Throw the ball," the image of the young Connor yelled.

Wrigley gave him a glance, then moved back to the rubber, stood a number of inches taller and threw the ball right handed with an old-fashioned, almost slow-motion Overall windup. The same highly effective pitch Orval Overall used to make the final out in the Cubbies' World-Series clinching game in 1908.

"Strikeeeeee!" yelled the umpire.

★ ★ ★

Annie sat in her chair out back enjoying a cup of tea. She was thinking how nice it'd been to see Wrigley growing up and spending more time with other kids.

She heard a loud bump on the side of the house. Annie rushed to the side door and grabbed the Louisville Slugger that was sitting right beside it. Whoever had knocked over the trashcans was struggling to get up. "Come on out, creep!" she screamed. Then she saw the long fingers trying to pull up the person attached to them. Annie rushed over to help Wrigley. "What in the world were you up to?"

"Nothing, Mom, nothing!" he interrupted, rushing to his feet, hiding his hands behind his back, looking guilty as sin. "I just uh…"

"Wrigs, what's behind your back?"

"What hands? I mean…"

"WRIGLEY!"

He showed the hand with the barely lit cigarette concealing the other hand.

"The other hand, too, son." He showed her the rest of the pack.

Annie closed the gap between her and Wrigley, took a deep breath, put a hand on his shoulder and grabbed him by the collar of his Ernie Banks jersey and got in his face.

"When did you start doing this?" she screamed, like the parent in an '80s *Just say no* commercial. It was almost comical. "What are you *thinking*? She continued to shake him until they both heard a rip.

"My jersey!" Wrigley screamed.

"Don't change the subject," she said, "Wrigley, what's going on with you?"

Wrigley looked down at his hands, sad and a little ashamed.

"You want to smoke?" Annie said, "*You want to smoke?!* Finish that one. Then light another, and another. You're finishing that pack!"

Wrigley thought that wasn't such a bad deal. He'd had two cigarettes before. He'd gotten a fresh pack from Black Patty: unfiltered Camels, the brand Black Patty's dad smoked.

Annie hovered over Wrigley while he finished his first cigarette. By the time Wrigley was done with the second cigarette, he was coughing.

"I think I'm done," Wrigley said. "I get it. I won't do it again."

"I don't think so, mister," said Annie. "In fact, *eat* the rest."

Wrigley looked up at Annie smiling. She wasn't returning the smile. "You're ah…kiddin', aren't you? *Mom?*"

"No, Wrigs. Cigarettes, booze, not on *my* clock." Annie said, and she began to choke up. "*Eat!*" she demanded.

He pulled a single cigarette from the pack, looked at it, and as the tears began to flow, he took a bite. His stomach flipped. His face started to turn a slight green color. He began to sob as he shoved the rest of the cigarette in his mouth and chomped away. "I need water," he managed to say as he held out the next cigarette at arm's length. Annie folded her arms and looked away, hiding tears of her own.

"Moooommmm," Wrigley begged, turning a darker green color. Annie couldn't do it anymore. She got up and went to the kitchen to get him some water. When she returned, Wrigley was passed out on the cement, with vomit all over his shirt.

"Oh, Christ," Annie moaned and gave him a shake. "Wrigley?...*Wrigley!*"

Wrigley came to, mumbling, "Leave me in for one more, coach…"

Annie smiled. She gently picked Wrigley up and walked him to the door. Inside, she wiped his face with a warm washcloth and guided him down the hallway to his room.

She stripped off his dirty shirt. She'd have some cleaning—and sewing—to do tonight. She put a Cubbie pajama top on him. He was mostly catatonic as she helped him change and gently placed him on his bed.

"You okay, buddy?" Annie asked, wiping his sweaty forehead.

"I quit," Wrigley said.

"Love you, Wrigs," Annie replied, kissing him on cheek.

"*Can't believe I made him do that,*" she whispered as she closed the door behind her, slightly horrified by her actions. Taking one last look at the snoring Wrigley, she smiled devilishly. *Just can't believe it.*

★ ★ ★

Before Connor had passed away, he'd built Wrigley a pitcher's mound. On the day he built it, as was his habit, Connor went after the project with a vengeance. He was up before sunrise outside in the backyard, working hard. Annie looked out the window, watching him move dirt with a wheelbarrow, building a large pile on the right side of the yard.

"Hey, you out there!" she yelled to Connor. "Hungry?"

Connor wiped the sweat form his brow and nodded emphatically. "Ooh! Yeah," he said, sounding exhausted. He came into the house and smelled pancakes, eggs, and bacon. He gave Annie a tight-lipped grin. She did the same.

"I'm sorry," Connor said, sitting down at the breakfast table. They had fought about Connor's drinking the night before. "I just gotta stop drinking, I know…*no more*," he said resolutely. Annie's smile faded and she looked down at her eggs. She'd heard this for years.

"Sweetie," Connor said softly, putting his hand on hers.

Annie was just about to give in when she pulled her hand away, got up from the table and stormed out of the room. By the end of the day, Connor had finished a regulation major league baseball mound, not unlike the mound he used to tend on Catalina Island for the Cubs. It had the same reddish colored dirt that had high clay content—and not a single pebble that could make a hard hit groundball take a bad hop and hurt a pitcher. Next, using plywood and two-by-fours, he created a four-by-eight-foot backstop. Then he attached Wrigley's orange-painted catcher's mitt to the wood with a few large screws, surrounding the whole backstop with soft netting to catch any balls that bounced off it. He thought either Wrigley would get a very satisfying pop when he hit the glove or a loud bang when the ball hit wood and fell to the ground. *Good mental conditioning*, he thought.

When he was done, he took one last gaze at the beautifully manicured piece of dirt and his mind wandered back, way back, to his 20th birthday, the night he had spent with Marilyn—a night that had ended up haunting him forever. Why hadn't he decided to go to Arizona and work for the Cubs? Why hadn't he listened to Marilyn when she had told him to follow his dream? Why didn't he call the number she had given him? While he knew such nights were fleeting, he had never been able to process the feelings he had felt that night and his lack of action. And no amount of alcohol would wash away his regrets.

'Tis better to have loved and lost, he thought. *Bullshit!*

CHAPTER 10

Wrigley looked to the stands; Koufax stood up. What was he doing in that crowd of old-time pitchers? But there he was, in living color. He held up his glove and gently turned it over, a motion pitchers use to signify curve. "Curve," Sandy said. And Wrigley heard him—loud and clear.

Donlin stepped back in, dug his cleats into the dirt, tapped his bat on the plate and focused hard on Wrigley's right hand. But what he saw confused him; he saw a glove. Wrigley had switched his mitt to his right hand to pitch lefty.

Wrigley closed his eyes, and as clear as if he were in Bubbs' den, heard the voice of Vin Scully: "There is something about a Sandy Koufax curve that just has to make you smile. When he rears back and lets it fly, you know most of the time it's just not going to get touched."

Wrigley put a little extra spin on the ball and felt his elbow snap, and for a brief moment it hurt like the old days before his operation.

"Strike twoooo!" yelled the umpire, admiring the perfect Koufax style twelve-to-six curve that had Donlin leaning way out of the box. Again, Donlin stepped out, looked at the dugout, where the bench coach for the Yankees furiously flipped through the rulebook.

Wrigley rubbed his left elbow, trying to release the tightness. The lone figure standing was still Sandy Koufax who signaled for a fastball. How many times had Wrigley thrown this pitch to Connor in his backyard to players from the past? How many times had he dreamt of this moment? He closed his eyes and listened.

"Folks," the voice of Vinny drawled in Wrigley's brain. "There is nothing more beautiful than a Sandy Koufax fastball. It is said to actually rise as it crosses the plate, which, for a hitter, makes it nearly impossible to touch."

Wrigley proceeded to wind up with the long, languid motion of Koufax in his prime. The ball catapulted through the air, rising just as it went over the inside corner of the plate. Donlin swung low and missed. Wrigley's elbow shocked him again with a painful jolt.

"Crap," Wrigley said, shaking out his arm.

★ ★ ★

Bubbs was in her chair, skinny, hunched over, a little shakier than years past, wearing a faded Cubs-blue checkered dress. She was straightening up her baseball cards on her side table, getting ready for the game, when Wrigley and Annie walked in.

"Hey, Bubbs," Wrigley said, waving and jumping onto his favorite couch. Even though he was now 16 years old, and getting bigger, thanks to Annie's genes, Wrigley still moved and sounded like a kid.

"What's for lunch?"

"Today we have sliced roast beef on homemade sourdough," Annie said with a flourish. "How's that sound, Bubbs?"

"If I had teeth, good," Bubbs said, searching around for her dentures. "Where the hell…?"

"I'll warm up some soup," Annie said, patting Bubbs' hand and leaving the room.

Bubbs almost fell asleep for a moment then turned toward Wrigley on the couch, startled, like she had just seen him for the first time.

"Hey Wrigs," Bubbs said, "did I ever tell you about my friend Billy Cianis. We called him Billy the Greek? Back in '45, Billy takes his goat to a Cubs game—boy did that goat stink! Let me tell you, nose-burning fumes! And he takes it right into Wrigley during the World Series. Last time the Cubbies had a shot. And Stan Jenkins, the usher, kicks Billy and his goat out of the park—" Bubbs stopped suddenly, closed her eyes, and not 10 seconds later, came back, "He had a *ticket* for the goat, but Stan kicks him out. Can't blame the guy—the goat smelled something awful! And Billy waves his arms and screams he's puttin' a curse on the Cubs. 'They'll never win a World Series!' he says, '*ever.*'" Bubbs glared at Wrigley like an old witch. Like she was putting a curse on *him*. Then she sat back in her chair and looked at the television.

"He shouldn't have said that," she said conclusively. "Our boys went on to lose to the Tigers in seven games—the closest they've ever gotten to winning the big one during my lifetime."

"I'm gonna take 'em there," Wrigley said under his breath. "Mom says so."

"Huh? You say something?" Bubbs growled.

"I *said*, 'I'm going to...'"

"It's a little hot, so wait," interrupted Annie, as she entered with a bowl of soup. "I have to get back to the oven. You two have fun."

★ ★ ★

That night, as Annie was saying goodnight to Wrigley, he told her about the Cubs/Dodgers game and how Bubbs had been busy with the dolls and messing with her cards and chants and how the Cubs won again, even though they didn't play so good.

"I think they have a shot, Mom," Wrigley said.

"I know they do," Annie said. "How's it going with the gang?"

"Oh, okay," Wrigley said. "Sometimes I feel kinda… *different*."

Annie brushed his cheek. "Did I ever tell you about Albert Spaulding?" Annie asked. "Talk about different. He was a Cubbie. I bet you didn't know that." Wrigley grinned, patting his pillow and laying his head down to listen. He hadn't heard *this* one before.

"Well, back in 1877, Spaulding…"

"1877? He was a Cub?" asked Wrigley, who knew very well there was no "Cubs" that year.

"Actually, they were called the White Stockings," said Annie, "*but* they would later *become* the Cubs."

"Just saying," Wrigley nodded, "please continue."

"Thank you," said Annie sarcastically. "Anyway, Albert Spaulding was a big strappin' man who used to pitch. When he started playing first base, his hands hurt when the ball came winging in. They didn't use gloves back then; do you believe that?"

"Wait, what?" Wrigley said, his mind blown.

"Didn't know any better. So Spaulding started making and wearing gloves. People used to think you were a wimp if you wore gloves, but here was this big dude that everybody respected, wearing one. He started making gloves in Chicago and selling them. Later, he became a famous sporting goods dealer, and he sold a ton of Spaulding gloves. They still make 'em today. Isn't that something?"

"Yeah," he said, thinking he could never play without his cherished ambi-glove. "Those guys were *tough*."

"Not as tough as you, Wrigs," Annie said, poking his nose.

"That was a super cool story, Mom," said Wrigley. "I'm not too old for bedtime stories, am I?"

"You never get too old for a good story," Annie said fluffing his pillow. She kissed his cheek. "Good night, Wrigs."

Wrigley smiled. "Good night."

★ ★ ★

"No, Bert," said Annie. "We're not going through this again."

"Aw, c'mon Annie," Bert responded. "I won't let him down this time. *I promise.*"

After another 20 minutes of persuasion, Annie gave in. She had to because Bert was Wrigley's father. "Fine," she sighed, "but I'm coming, too. And *you're* buying the Cracker Jack."

A week later, the three were sitting in the left field bleachers at Wrigley Field. Annie stuck out her hand. Burt put a few dollars and some loose change in it. She looked down at her hand with slight disgust. "What?" said Bert, "It's all I've got. And remember, *I* bought the tickets."

Annie held her tongue and headed off to the snack stand. Bert leaned in to Wrigley. "So," he said, "you really thinking of trying to go pro?"

"Dad," Wrigley rolled his eyes. "I've been planning on going pro since I was three."

Wrigley was sitting on the bench where he was born. Bert looked disapprovingly at his glove and felt a scalding hot "E" on his forehead. He took a long drink from his beer.

"You're sixteen," Bert said.

"Duh."

"Well, uh," Bert looked away, "I think it's time you got real about baseball and life, son."

"What do you mean?" Wrigley asked, looking out on to the field of his namesake, waiting for the game to start.

"Oh, Wrigley. Your mom has been filling you with pipe dreams about being a professional pitcher since you were a baby. I don't know why. I should have stopped her years ago."

"Why?" Wrigley responded, not sure where his dad was going with this.

"I know you can see better now and think you got a shot."

"Why not?" Wrigley said.

"Thousands of kids who have been pitching their whole lives and seeing their whole lives…. Well, they've got a lot better chance than you."

Wrigley looked at his dad like an intruder. "I'm gonna be a closer."

"Sorry, Wrigs, but it's just the facts, and I bet deep inside you know it."

Wrigley wanted to pound him into dust. Who was this lazy bum to tell *him* what kind of chance he had to do *anything*? He rifled through the salty vocabulary he acquired from the Lasaine Gang, and through tight lips, settled on, "anything can happen." He turned to hide the tears welling in his eyes as he started rocking and pounding his mitt, left-handed then right-handed.

"I just don't want to see you hurt," Bert said, still feeling like he was doing Wrigley a service.

Annie came back with three popcorns and some hotdogs. "Not enough money for Cracker Jack," she said sarcastically, then saw Wrigley wiping his face with his glove.

"What you two talkin' about?" Annie innocently asked.

"The kid's head is full of pipe dreams, Annie," Bert said. "Just trying to talk a little sense into him."

Annie looked at Wrigley, who stopped rocking, but kept pounding his mitt, his cheeks streaked with tears.

"What *kind* of sense?" Annie asked, knowing *exactly* what Bert meant.

"The truth, Annie," he said, then looking at her condescendingly, "the *truth*."

"When's the last time you've seen your own son pitch?" she asked. Bert's cheeks flushed. "*When?*"

"That's…that's not fair, Annie," Bert responded, looking out on to the field.

"Oh no?" her eyes were locked in. "Where the hell have you been the last 8 years? Hell, make that 10!"

"Annie," Bert said in a softer voice, looking around at the bleacher bums, embarrassed. "Not here. Not now."

"Oh this is happening," she said, still holding the food. "*Now*."

Wrigley focused on the precariously balanced tray he thought would go flying. He was suddenly hungry.

Bert made a "settle down" gesture with his hands, which angered Annie more. "You're a jerk, Bert Sanders, a real ass," she yelled. A number of people were now staring at her. She didn't care. "I don't even know what I was thinking coming here," Annie said, almost to herself. She started to speak calmly. "You haven't changed, Bert Sanders."

"Annie, I…" Bert stared, cutting her off.

"Save it!" said Annie, then, handed the food to Bert, who sheepishly took it from her. She took Wrigley's hand, "C'mon, Wrigs, we're out of here."

"But the game, Mom," Wrigley said, with a pleading look. "The food?"

Annie looked down at Wrigley, wiped a tear off his cheek, turned back to Bert and angrily grabbed the tray of food. "Give me that," Annie said to Bert, who was suddenly speechless.

Annie nodded for Wrigley to follow and they headed up the stairs of the bleachers.

"The only good thing I got out of being with him was you," Annie said to Wrigley as they spotted two seats about 20 rows above Bert. "And *that* I'm very thankful for. Let's just enjoy the rest of this game, the food, and forget about what happened. Okay?"

"Okay."

After Wrigley calmed down, he realized he had a great view of Turk Wendell warming up in the Cubs' bullpen. He wondered how he must be feeling, thinking *I can't wait 'til that's me.*

CHAPTER 11

"Strike out number one for Wrigley," said Vin Scully in the booth. "He keeps that up, he's gonna mow them down like soft spring grass under a John Deere."

Wrigley turned to Sandy, who smiled, waved with a nod, and sat down. Wrigley started looking into the stands for his next pitcher.

"He can't do *that*," yelled the Yankees' manager.

"What?" said the umpire.

"Pitch with both arms," the manager yelled.

"He just did," joked the ump, then quickly smiled and said, "Hold on, hold on."

"I think we may have a problem folks," said Vinny. "I don't know if you noticed, but Wrigley Sanders switched arms in the middle of a batter. I believe under the Venditte rule that is a legal move. Let's wait and see what the umpires say."

"This is not a circus! It's the friggin' World Series," the manager yelled.

"Really, Mac? I hadn't noticed," said the umpire, as he turned to the crew chief at third base.

★ ★ ★

After the game, Wrigley was up late in his bedroom, rocking back and forth, banging his head against the wall. Annie heard the noise and slowly walked toward Wrigley's bedroom. She opened the door and there he was, dressed in his Cubbie jammies, eyes closed, rocking back and forth. Then, *slam!*

"Wrigley, what's up," Annie asked trying to sound casual. "Is it about Dad being an ass at the game?"

Wrigley didn't respond, just eyeing her and continuing to rock forward, and backward, and ending with a boom!

"Okay then. If you're going to be that way, I'm not going to call that pitching coach Papa recommended."

Wrigley stopped dead in his tracks, blinked a few times, and asked, "What pitching coach?"

"Papa left me a note. Told me when I thought you were ready to try out for the Cubs that I should call him."

"The Cubs? The Cubs!" said Wrigley, shaking his head, rocking a little again, picking up his mitt and slamming the right side, switching and slamming the left. "I just want to be ready to try out for the high school team."

"Huh?" Annie said, as she moved closer to Wrigley and noticed a piece of paper—a tryout notice for the high school team. "What?"

"High school, Mom." Wrigley said, holding up the notice. "I'm not ready for the Cubbies—yet."

"Oh," said Annie, then started to laugh.

At first, Wrigley didn't get it, but soon he realized his mom had been worried sick about him being pissed at his dad, and truthfully, it was just a high school tryout that was stressing him out. He couldn't help it. He'd never really thought he would get to pitch, not even at a high school. When he'd seen the tryout notice, he'd had a full-blown panic attack. At least that was what he thought it was. His heart had raced and he was scared, but he didn't know what he was afraid of. Maybe he just wasn't sure if he was good enough?

"Wrigs, you're good enough," Annie said, like she was reading his mind. She had been reading his face—as clearly as the words in a book.

"I don't know," Wrigley said, stopping the rocking and starting to relax a little.

"I'll make sure you're ready. I'll call Papa's friend. He'll get you ready, okay?"

For the first time, a small grin broke out on Wrigley's face and grew larger and larger until he was nearly laughing when he said, "That'd be swell Mom. Just swell!"

★ ★ ★

The next morning Annie made the call.

"Sure. I'd love to meet the young man," Rudy Jones said on the phone. "I made a promise to Connor I'd take good care of him. Always keep my word."

"Thank you so much, Mr. Jones," Annie said. "I was thinking maybe at the high school? He's hoping to pitch for them."

"Let's schedule for Saturday at 10:00 a.m. North field. Tell Wrigley to bring his glove and a new ball," Rudy said. "Annie," he continued, taking on a solemn tone, "your dad is why I made it as a pitching coach in the majors. He was a genius when it came to coaching. And the most generous guy I ever knew. He was a great man."

"Thank you," Annie said, grateful. "Wrigley will be there Saturday, 10:00 a.m., Mr. Jones."

"*Rudy*," he responded.

"Rudy," she said.

Wrigley peddled his bike to the high school dressed in full Cubbie regalia, complete with his 1908 grey and black hat. When he arrived at the field he saw a tall—and to his young eyes, old—skinny black man sitting in the bleachers, wearing a grey pinstriped suit reading the New York Times sports page.

"Rudy?" Wrigley asked, sneaking up to him.

"Wrigley!" Toothpick said, having some trouble folding the newspaper and opting to crumple it up and put it beside him. He stuck out his hand for shaking. "You can call me Toothpick. That's what your grandpa called me."

Wrigley squinted at him. His mouth dropped open. "Toothpick *Jones*?" he blurted out. "*The* Toothpick Jones? Papa told me about you…the night before…he died…"

"Not *that* Toothpick," Rudy said, like his young charge was silly to even suggest it. "Toothpick Jones died in '71."

"Oh—ohh," Wrigley said nodding, realizing this old man looked a bit young for his grandpa's story.

"Some say I resemble him," Toothpick said. "Some of my friends, like your grandpa, gave me the nickname. You can call me that if you like. I always respected your grandpa. A true baseball man."

"Taught me everything I know," Wrigley said, looking down at his mitt, giving it a couple of pounds, feeling a heaviness on his chest.

Toothpick cracked a crooked, sympathetic smile. "That's a *fine* uniform, son—and a nice pair of glasses. Shave off those curls, and you'd be a dead ringer for Ryne Duren."

"Ryne Duren?" Wrigley asked.

"That guy," Rudy said, shaking his head. "Hitters couldn't see his fastball. And *he* couldn't see *them*. Casey Stengel said, 'If he ever hit you in the head, you might be in the past tense.'" Rudy made a big funny face. Wrigley started laughing.

"Thatta boy," said Toothpick. "How bout we do some pitching?" He jumped off his bleacher and guided Wrigley toward the pitcher's mound. On the way there, he noticed the ambi-glove. "That's an different glove."

"It's an ambi," Wrigley responded brightly. "Papa had it made for me so I can throw right- *and* left-handed.

"No kidding?" Toothpick said, stopping at the foul line taking Wrigley in. This kid was something else. Wrigley just looked up at him, waiting, not sure about the soft look Toothpick was giving him. Toothpick came back, put his hand on Wrigley's shoulder and warmly coaxed him to the mound.

"I like to start off each session with a question," Toothpick said when they got there. "I believe a winning pitcher is a *smart* pitcher. This might be a hard one, but can you tell me who has won the 1992 Cy Young award?"

"Tssssh," Wrigley smiled. "Greg Maddux as a Cub, then as a Brave in '93 and '94, and I bet he wins it this year too!"

"Well done," said Toothpick. "Why do you think Maddux pitches so well?" Toothpick asked.

"Well…" Wrigley said, scratching the mound with his cleats. Toothpick noticed how old they looked. *Bet those were Connor's*, he thought. "He can put the ball wherever he wants. He's not overpowering but has a nice spread between his heater and curve."

"He's *smart*," said Toothpick, poking Wrigley's temple twice. "He's unpredictable, and he knows the patterns of his hitters. That's something we are going to work on today." Toothpick pulled a ball from his jacket pocket and put it in Wrigley's glove. He then pulled a catcher's mitt out of his back pocket. Wrigley wasn't sure how he fit it in there. Toothpick noticed Wrigley's confused face, like a kid at a magic show and laughed before hustling back behind the plate.

"Okay, nice and easy, son," Toothpick said squatting. "Your mom tells me you're a closer, so let's start off smokin'. Give me your heater." Then, noticing Wrigley licking his chops, "But go easy at first."

Wrigley threw a few fastballs from his standard windup using his right arm. Then he switched it up and used his left-handed Sandy Koufax windup, which Rudy estimated added five extra miles per hour to his pitch.

"That's the one!" he called out. "Nice pitch. Hmm, Sandy Koufax. Connor taught you well," Toothpick said.

"How about a curve?" Wrigley said.

Before Toothpick could say anything, in came a curve that looked like it was released from the arm of Koufax. The bottom dropped off the pitch and it landed a few inches from the ground.

"Wait, wait, wait," said Toothpick, standing up in disbelief. "I just realized you threw from the left side."

"Well, *yeah*, why not?" Wrigley said, like it was the most obvious thing in the world.

"When you said you threw from both sides, I didn't think…" Toothpick trailed off. The kid looked at him like *he* was the crazy one. "Your pitch…that was a perfectly executed Koufax curve if I've ever seen one," Toothpick said.

"Thank you," said Wrigley. "Wanna see my drop ball?"

Leave it to Connor, Toothpick thought, laughing to himself. "Absolutely."

He squatted back down behind the plate and held up a hand to indicate he needed a moment to get back down there. Toothpick nodded and got ready. Wrigley wound up, doing his best right-handed imitation of Orval Overall, pulled it off, but it hit about a foot before the plate. Toothpick tried his best to catch it but missed it.

"Darn," said Wrigley.

"That…*disappeared*," said Toothpick as he ran after the ball. "If you can control it, that's your right-handed strike out pitch."

"Still needs a little work," Wrigley said.

"That's *okay*?" Toothpick said, not entirely sure what he was witnessing as he threw the ball back to Wrigley. Seeing Wrigley's disappointment in his pitch, Toothpick realized his young Padawan was for real. "Pitching is complicated," he said, trying to comfort him. "Let me see your right-handed windup—in slow motion."

"Sure thing," Wrigley said and did his windup in slow motion, and just when his front foot hit the ground Toothpick said, "Freeze! See that?"

Wrigley looked down. He didn't see anything out of the ordinary.

"First of all, your foot is not pointing directly to the catcher," Toothpick said. "It's pointing toward third base. That is going to reduce your velocity. Second, your front leg is not landing solid. It's giving in, which again affects your velocity. I want you to land like this…"

Toothpick did a windup and came down with his right foot pointing perfectly to home plate "See my back toe," he said, "…it helps keep my front leg solid. No drift. So I can whip around and get more torque."

Wrigley tried the motion once, then again. Toothpick watched and nodded his approval.

"That's it," Toothpick said.

"Can I throw a few?" he asked.

"Sure."

Wrigley tossed a few pitches and the ball came out of his hand smooth and easy, with a ton more velocity.

"Wow," Wrigley said, feeling the effect in his body *and* hearing the pop of Toothpick's glove. "That's *amazing*. Thanks! What else can I work on?"

"I like your spirit," Toothpick said. "Work on that this week. There may be a few more things we can tweak along the way, but start there. Don't want your head to explode."

"I can handle it today, I promise!" said Wrigley, begging. "I like to work hard."

"It shows," said Toothpick, walking to the mound. "You really want to be successful, Wrigley?"

"I do, I do!" Wrigley said, eager as a puppy. "I promised my grandpa I'd try. I'm gonna do it. Besides, Mom says I can take the Cubs to the World Series."

Toothpick smiled. "Okay, Wrigs. I want you to continue to dream—all the great ones do that. And they all have a love of winning, a drive to exceed, and I believe you have that too."

Wrigley felt a warmth he hadn't experienced since he was in the presence of his grandpa. He went from being disappointed to feeling something that was far stronger when the lesson had ended. He reached out to thank Toothpick with his left hand. "Thanks Rudy," Wrigley said.

"Call me Toothpick," he said again, smiling, returning the shake. Toothpick was startled when he realized how big and strong Wrigley's hands were.

"Impressive hands," he said. Then he took a deep breath and looked around, like he was making sure no one was looking. "How about one more lesson?"

Wrigley's eyes got big. "Yes, yes!"

"Look at the ball," he said. "Do you see anything *special* about it?"

Wrigley turned it over in his hand. "It's, uh, *new?*"

"I'm talking about the way it sits in your hand," Toothpick said.

Toothpick gently turned the ball in Wrigley's hand so he held his middle finger on the inside of the seams.

"Curveball," said Wrigley

"Show me your fastball grip," Toothpick said. Wrigley complied.

"Here's the deal," said Toothpick. "That's a decent fast ball grip. I have some other options we can work on. But for now, I want you to toss the ball up in the air, catch it, and spin it to a curveball, fastball, or changeup grip—a different spin each time."

"Okay," Wrigley said.

"You don't want to tip your pitches. In the pros, guys in the dugout are watching your every move. Say you want to throw a curve; even before you get your sign, just catch it and go to that grip. You just have to mix it up so they don't find a pattern."

"I'll do that every day from now on—every day," said Wrigley, holding the ball close to his face, scrutinizing it.

"One more thing," said Toothpick. "Pitch with your heart not your eyes."

"Huh?" Wrigley said, continuing to observe the ball like it was the first time he had seen one.

"Watch this windup," Toothpick said, trying to get Wrigley's attention, "who is it?" He went into a windup with his eyes going up to the sky and then back down as he threw the ball.

"Fernando," Wrigley smiled. "I just used that not long ago."

"Really? Wow," Toothpick said in amazement. "Fernando Valenzuela was just one of the greats, and I could name dozens, who pitched with their heart, not their eyes. I know you can see well enough now, but," Toothpick paused, about to go deep, "I want you to practice pitching with your eyes closed."

"Toothpick," said Wrigley pointing to his glasses, "I've been pitching that way most of my life."

"I was thinking that might be the case," said Toothpick, putting a hand on Wrigley's shoulder.

Toothpick looked at his watch. "Okay, that's enough for today. I'll come by your place 7 a.m. tomorrow and we'll get to work."

"I'll be in full uniform," Wrigley said excited.

"Wear shorts and sandals," Toothpick said. Wrigley looked confused. Toothpick looked him in the eye. "*Trust* me. See you at seven—*sharp*."

★ ★ ★

At 6:58 a.m., Toothpick was at Wrigley's house, knocking on the door wearing shorts, Teva sandals, and a fly-fishing vest.

"We going fishing?" asked Wrigley.

"Not exactly," Toothpick said, smiling. "We're headed to the ball field." Wrigley shrugged his shoulders and followed Toothpick to his sleek, black BMW.

"Balance Wrigley balance," Toothpick said as they drove, his eyes squarely on the road. "Balance and control are everything in pitching. My dad was a great pitcher, a fine man, and one thing he stressed to me was the importance of balance."

"Can I ask you something?" Wrigley said.

"Sure," Toothpick responded.

"Why didn't *you* ever pitch in the Bigs?"

"Lack of balance," Toothpick said, with a sad laugh. "My dad was a great teacher. I'm not sure I was a very good student."

"What happened?"

"Well," started Toothpick, thinking about how to answer, "I had a rocket arm with exceptional stuff, but I…I blew it out trying to impress my dad."

Toothpick squinted at the horizon. "I wasn't even pitching for me. I was pitching for him." Toothpick looked at Wrigley. "Who are *you* pitching for Wrigley?"

Wrigley didn't quite understand, but he flashed through pictures of pitching to his grandpa; the conversation with his dad at the Cubs game; and his mom throwing a baseball from the left field bleachers, though for this last image he had no context—it was kind of surreal. He knew the answer Toothpick wanted to hear. "For me?"

"Knowing why you do something is important, Wrigley," Toothpick said. "*Why* matters."

They pulled into the parking lot and Toothpick unloaded a few delicate-looking fly rods from the trunk.

"Could you please grab those rings," Toothpick said, motioning to a number of colorful plastic rings in various diameters from a foot to three feet.

"Sure," Wrigley said.

They walked out to the outfield.

"Here's the deal son," Toothpick said, "set the biggest one about 40 feet away and we'll see what we're made of…"

"Got it," Wrigley said.

Toothpick quickly put together two fly rods and tied pieces of red yarn at the end of the line.

"Here," Toothpick said, handing Wrigley a rod. "Watch me now."

Toothpick held the rod up high above his head, gently raising his right arm back with the line following behind him. He gently moved his right arm forward, stopping just past his ear. The bend of the rod gently catapulted the yarn out into the ring, softly landing right in the middle.

Wrigley stared in disbelief.

"*Your* turn," Toothpick said, smiling. Wrigley looked at him like he was crazy. "Go on."

Wrigley cautiously moved the rod back and forth, and the line barely went anywhere.

"I don't get it," Wrigley said. "How do you *do* that?"

"Watch," Toothpick said. Toothpick reared back his fly rod, went forward in a slow, elegant fashion, stopped his arm like he was hammering a nail into a wall, and the fly line gently floated into the big ring. "Load. Relax…wait for it…release." He brought the rod back, relaxed, then brought it forward during each cast. It was slow, beautiful, and powerful.

Wrigley tried to relax but he reared back, whipped the line behind his head with a loud *snap*, and whipped the line forward to make a cool *pop*. When he tried to stop at the end, his arm kept on going and the line went limp just five feet in front of him.

Toothpick's stifled laughter hit Wrigley worse than if he had rolled around in hysterics. "Crap," Wrigley said to himself, looking at the fly rod. "Load, relax, release…Crap."

"You can do it," Toothpick said. "You have to stop the rod, like you're pounding a nail into a wall…or flinging peanut butter off a spoon. That'll catapult the fly line."

Toothpick understood that Wrigley didn't get it. "It's something you have to experience," he said.

"How can I experience it if I haven't experienced it?" It sounded funny coming out of his mouth, but it made Toothpick light up.

"Exactly!" said Toothpick. Wrigley knew he had said something right, but he wasn't sure what, and all he was left with was this limp line.

"It's cool that you can do that," said Wrigley, "but I'm not a fisherman, I'm a pitcher, and I'm not sure…"

"You practice this every day for a week," said Toothpick cutting him off. "If you give me your commitment that you'll try *every day* for 20 minutes, and you still can't find it, we'll retire the lesson."

Wrigley shrugged and nodded.

"One more thing," said Toothpick. "No pitching until I see you again."

Wrigley's eyes went big, horrified. "What?!"

"No throwing a baseball, no windups, no baseball. Only outfield fly-fishing."

Wrigley motioned to object, but Toothpick put a finger to his own lips. "That's enough for today, you have your assignment."

★ ★ ★

Exactly one week later, after going to the park every morning, Wrigley finally got the hang of tossing the fly rod. He'd thought of quitting more than once. But he persevered, because he was stubborn, at least that's what his grandpa had once told him. If he kept his wrist stiff through the whole process, waited for the line to go all the way behind him, then moved forward with a steady movement, then abruptly stopped, the line would gently land right where he aimed it.

The first time he successfully did it he yelled so loud he woke up a sleeping transient. The second, then the third time, it got even easier. And soon, it became a habit. Right from the park, he called Toothpick and reported his success, telling him he'd figured out the secret to outfield fly-fishing.

"Great," Toothpick said. I'll be there in half an hour. I want to see this for myself."

Twenty-five minutes later Toothpick came walking out toward Wrigley with a baseball home plate in his hand.

"Now what?" Wrigley said. "You gonna make me hit that?"

"As a matter of fact, just the opposite," Toothpick said, as he started to nail a big piece of black Velcro-faced material onto the wood handball backstop. He mounted the home plate right in the middle of the black about two feet off the ground. He walked about 50 feet from the target and started casting his fly rod, hitting to the right and left of the plate, with the yarn actually sticking onto the Velcro upon contact. "Never hit the plate son, never."

Wrigley cast elegantly: loaded, relaxed, and released his yarn sticking it right next to the plate.

"Nicely done," Toothpick said, pulling out a piece of black cloth and said, "You're ready for the next level."

He removed Wrigley's glasses, put them in his shirt pocket and gently placed a blindfold over his eyes. "Take one quick peak, put the blindfold back on and imagine the target. Then let it fly."

Wrigley squinted at Toothpick, and not because he was trying to adjust his eyes. "Go on," said Toothpick tilting his head toward the non-target.

Wrigley said, "Going for the inside right." Then he cast.

"Take a peek," Toothpick said.

Wrigley lifted the blindfold off his eyes and squinted as Toothpick handed him his glasses.

"I got it!" Wrigley said.

"Go for the outside corner," Toothpick said.

Wrigley looked at the outside corner, handed Toothpick his glasses without breaking his focus, then put on the blindfold and cast. Wrigley started to take off the blindfold.

"Wait! Keep it on! Trust me that you got it. Now I want you to cast again, using your left arm, aiming for the *inside* corner."

"Can I look?" Wrigley protested.

"Just load, relax, and release." Toothpick said, and raising his voice just a little, "Now *cast!*"

Wrigley switched hands and cast the rod left-handed. "Did I hit it?

Silence.

"Did I?"

"Take a look," said Toothpick. Wrigley ripped off his blindfold. It was a bull's eye!

"Tomorrow," Toothpick said smiling, "We use a baseball and a mitt."

★ ★ ★

"'Night, Coach," said Wrigley as he exited the car.

"'Night, Wrigs," said Toothpick smiling. Wrigley closed the car door and ran to the front door of his house.

"Hey, Wrigs," Toothpick called out through the passenger window. Wrigley turned around. "Come back for a sec."

Wrigley jogged back to the car and rested his arms on the car door. "What's up?"

Toothpick got real serious. "Did you think of why you want to pitch?"

"Yeah," he said reflecting Toothpick's seriousness, "yeah, I did."

"And?"

"C'mon!" Wrigley broke out in to a big smile. "I want to help the Cubs win the World Series! Because, well, Mom said I could."

Toothpick solemn face broke out in to a big smile. "Mom said…I'll take that," he said. "Now go rest that arm—*both* of them."

CHAPTER 12

The umpire and the crew chief huddled near the mound, while the Cubs manager stood tapping his shoe on the dirt just ten feet away.

"This is going to take some time, folks," Vin Scully drawled from the broadcast booth, "because the rules regarding pitching from both sides have some dust on them. In the meantime, Wrigley Sanders has one heck of a story. His grandfather worked for the Cubbies back when they had spring training on Catalina Island back in the fifties. Imagine what it was like to leave cold, snowy Chicago and come west to a warm, sunny paradise. Yup, the Wrigleys of chewing gum fame owned the island, and it was one little bit of spring training paradise with lots of fishing, sunning—even sailing. More later. It looks like they may have figured it out."

The crew chief clearly and concisely told both managers and a few players, "This is covered in the Venditte rule. The pitcher starts by indicating which arm he is pitching with; once he puts his foot on the rubber, that's your side. Then the hitter decides what side; each one gets to change only once. No rules were broken. The hitter is out." And he made a dramatic out sign.

Wrigley started to feel ill again. He tried deep breathing, complete with a few long "paa paa" sounds. "Get it together, Wrigs, get it to…" and with that, he leaned over the back of the mound and threw up.

The trainer immediately jogged to the mound. Wrigley's hands were on his knees and he was staring straight down.

"What's up?" he asked Wrigley, putting a hand on his back.

"Stomach feels better now," Wrigley said craning his head. "Give me a second." Wrigley stood up and stretched his arms across his body. Right first, then left. He winced dramatically.

"Which arm?" the trainer asked.

"Ah, I may not be able to throw lefty," Wrigley said. "I hurt something."

The trainer examined Wrigley's arm. "How long ago was the operation?"

"Fourteen, fifteen years ago," Wrigley said.

The trainer messaged the elbow, then gently stretched Wrigley's left arm. The pain that shot through was so unbearable he growled like a wounded animal.

"Jeeezzzz! Better stay with your right side," said the trainer.

Wrigley shook his head "yes" and looked back at the outfield fences. That's when he noticed there was no ivy on the fences. He shook his head and looked again; still no ivy. He figured he was concussed, or maybe it was the effect of the nasty pain he was experiencing. He had to just walk it off, but when he turned back to look at the plate, he saw the Sultan of Swat walking to the batter's box, rotund, confident, staring him down.

What year is this? Wrigley thought to himself. *Is that really Babe Ruth?*

★ ★ ★

Toothpick and Annie watched as Wrigley took the mound for the first time with the varsity high school team. His catcher, Martin Prior, was a tall, lean kid with a ready smile. He came out with Wrigley's orange catcher's mitt. The first batter up hit from the right side. He had a short, quick swing—a contact hitter. Martin called for a fastball. Wrigley took a moment, whispered the word "Papa," then wound up, using his Koufax motion, and whipped a heater just on the inside of the plate.

"Strike one!" yelled the umpire.

The hitter nervously tapped the plate a few times. Martin called for a curve. Wrigley obliged with a beautiful Koufax curve that grazed the other side of the plate. The batter swung and missed by a mile. Strike two. In the stands, Annie's face was turning red. She had not taken a breath since the first pitch. Toothpick noticed. He reached over and jabbed her lightly with his elbow. "Breathe," he said. "He's doing fine."

The batter was out of the box, cleaning the dirt off his cleats, not in a hurry to hit against this weird-looking kid with nasty stuff. Wrigley switched his mitt back and forth popping his mitt with alternate hands.

"Let's go," said the umpire.

The batter put one foot back in the batter's box and looked at Martin behind the plate. Martin whispered, "I wouldn't want to hit against him either," then chuckled.

Finally, the batter entered the batter's box with the second foot and tapped the plate. Martin gave Wrigley the sign calling for the ol' number one.

Wrigley smiled, nodded, went into his windup, and threw a Nolan Ryan fastball with his right hand that seemed to cross the plate before the batter brought the bat off his shoulder.

"Strike three!"

The crowd, all 13 of it, cheered as Wrigley stood on the mound and instinctively tipped his cap. On the sidelines, the coach from the other team was thumbing through a rulebook. His assistant coach was jabbering in his ear. Toothpick saw this. "Oh boy," he whispered, not good."

"What?" Annie said.

"I think they noticed Wrigley threw with both arms," he said, nodding toward the visitors' dugout. Just then the coach of the opposing team called time and walked out to the umpire. Toothpick ran to the fence to get closer to the conversation and drove his ear between the links, trying to hear what was being said.

"I can't find the rule, but I think it's illegal to use a catcher's glove that's painted orange," said the coach.

The umpire looked back at Martin and his orange glove, saying, "I hadn't even noticed."

The umpire waved to Wrigley's coach named Hayho, who came trotting out. They met each other at the first-base line.

"Whew," said Toothpick to himself.

"What is it?" asked Annie. She had followed Toothpick down.

Startled, he turned around. "Oh, nothing," he said smiling. "At least it's not what I thought it was."

"What is it then?" she asked.

"Oh it's just something about the catcher's glove and the orange-painted rim," he said, wiping his brow with relief. But Annie understood that this glove was important to Wrigley and interrupted the meeting between the coaches and umpire. "Yo!" she screamed.

The umpire and coaches turned around. "There's no rule that outlaws orange, unless the glove is waved and it distracts the batter!"

The umpire looked up at Annie. "Who's that?" he asked Coach Hayho.

"The pitcher's mom," Hayho said, laughing. "She knows the rules better than I do."

The umpire looked at the visiting team's coach, "You okay with that?" he asked, not wanting to scrutinize the rule book any further.

The visiting coach looked back at Annie, who not only looked confident, but ready to brawl.

"Yeah, yeah. Sure," he said, worried the fence might not hold mama bear if he gave any further protest.

"Good," said the umpire. Then, turning to Martin and Coach Hayho, "Make sure he doesn't distract the hitters with the mitt, and we'll stick with this glove."

"Will do," said coach Hayho, offering a two-finger salute and running off the field. He gave Annie a friendly wave of the hand.

The next hitter was a large lefty. He came to the plate, took one long smooth swing, spat on the plate, and dug in, all the while keeping his eyes sharply on Wrigley.

Martin turned to the umpire. "Time out."

"Make it quick," the umpire said, looking at his watch.

Martin ran out to the mound. "Wrigs," he said looking back at the hitter, "What do you think?"

"Maddux," said Wrigley, squinting his eyes at the batter.

Martin smiled. "Good call, Wrigs. Keep moving the ball around." Wrigley nodded. "Work the edges, but if he doesn't bite and the ump isn't giving you the call, *walk him*."

Wrigley's first pitch was about four inches off the plate, perfect, but the big lefty reached out and smacked it on the ground to the left side of Wrigley. Wrigley tried to snag the ball but missed and it rolled in to the outfield for a single. Wrigley pounded the inside of his glove. *Just missed*, he thought to himself as he collected the ball from the second baseman.

Martin tilted his head and opened his hands—a look that said, "*It could've been worse.*" Wrigley nodded in agreement and let that one go.

The next hitter was a stocky right-hander with a very compact practice swing. He had a similarly confident look to the previous batter—he was anxious to rip the ball—but Martin wasn't so worried about him parking one. Martin put down a fastball; Wrigley shook it off. He put down a curve; Wrigley shook it off. Martin frustratingly put down three fingers.

Changeup. Wrigley nodded, closed his eyes and wound up just exactly like he did for his Nolan Ryan fastball. The stocky hitter assumed he knew what was coming and swung so early and so hard that he almost came out of his shoes. Martin repeated his series of signs and Wrigley chose the changeup again. The hitter was fooled again. The third pitch was a no brainer for Wrigley—a fastball. He knew the hitter might be thinking no way would he throw three changeups in a row, but he did throw two; maybe he would, maybe he wouldn't. He had the hitter right where he wanted him—completely befuddled. It was the perfect setup for a low fastball to induce a double play ball. Wrigley kept the ball down and just a little tight, and the hitter swung hard but hit it right to the shortstop for an inning ending double play. Annie and Toothpick embraced, Annie with tears in her eyes. "He did it," Toothpick whispered into her ear. "Your son did it."

★ ★ ★

He looked around the field, and playing behind him was the most famous double play combination in the history of the game—Tinkers to Evers to Chance. *Are you kiddin' me? What is going on here? Am I pitching for the Cubs in the 1932 World Series?*

Wrigley looked back in toward the plate. Connor put down the signal for a fastball. Wrigley put the mitt on his left hand, ready to pitch righty. But Ruth was a lefty, and a good one at that. He switched his mitt and patted the pocket.

He went back and forth a few more times, not sure which side to use. The umpire raised his hands to signal a time out and started walking to the mound. Wrigley was now rocking back and forth, switching mitts, in a confused trance.

"Pick a side. And let's go," yelled the umpire.

"Well folks," Vin Scully said, "Wrigley Sanders is talking himself through the decision of a lifetime—which arm to use. He's not the first pitcher to use self-talk to get through a tough situation. But I must admit this is a new conundrum. Lefty. Righty. By all accounts, his left arm looks hurt. Oh boy. He's toeing the rubber as a lefty. Here we go; hold on to your horses."

CHAPTER 13

Wrigley, with fake I.D. and his bushy hair and mustache, looked much older than the other kids. He walked into the liquor store.

"Who you buying the Schnapps for kid?" a man asked Wrigley on his way out.

Oh shit, he thought, as he saw a badge on the man's hip. "State Alcohol Agent," it read.

"For my dad," he managed, but his defeated tone was a signed confession.

"I'm betting on a few friends outside," said a second man coming up behind him. Wrigley, a paper bag in each arm, looked behind him to see another hip badge, then followed the jeans and brown t-shirt up to a green John Deere trucker hat.

"Shall we?" said the first agent, holding the door for Wrigley. Wrigley walked slowly out the door, then *bolted*. Outside were Biggs, George, Monty Jack, Black Patty, and Elliott practically waiting for the relay. Biggs in the driver's seat of his 1964 Mustang, Elliott riding shotgun, and Monty Jack waiting by the passenger side rear door like a chauffeur. George and Black Patty were waiting by the door to help Wrigley carry the booze.

George and Black Patty, running alongside Wrigley, who seemed more concerned about not dropping the booze than the pursuit, each took a bag off his hands and made for the car.

"Jump in!" Biggs said, as Monty Jack first let George and Black Patty in the car before jumping in himself. Wrigley felt a sharp tug on his collar and fell backward to the ground.

The gang pulled out of the parking lot skidding their tires.

"*Some* friends," said one of the agents as they stared down at Wrigley.

"Well, I…uh…" Wrigley said, fishing for words. "Crap," he said and held out his hands for the inevitable cuffs.

"Listen kid," said the agent, yanking Wrigley up to his feet, "just don't do it again, okay? We'll let you off this time."

"Thanks, officer," said Wrigley, still not sure this was going to be the end of it, but not wanting to push his luck, started to walk away.

"Hey kid!" the first agent yelled out. *I knew it wouldn't be that easy*, Wrigley thought as he slowly turned around. "Some words of advice: take it easy with the sauce, okay. You look like a good kid. You hear what I'm saying?"

"Yes, sir," Wrigley said, smiling.

★ ★ ★

That night they all drank the beer, sucking down a can, chasing it with a shot of Peppermint Schnapps. The booze was exacerbating the sadness Wrigley felt after being ditched.

"Putney Swope says you got to have soul!" yelled Elliott as he tossed his final beer can over his shoulder and stood up from the curb. He started jogging around in circles and stretching out his legs like he was getting ready for a race. All the gang stood up, hooting and hollering and started jogging too. Wrigley followed, not knowing what the heck was going on.

Soon, they were running down side streets and came upon the main street of Vanowen Avenue. On the right stood five apartment buildings built in the fifties. Small planter boxes were out front. Four-foot-high wood fences surrounded the patio apartments on the ground level.

"Putney Swope says you got to have soul!" Elliott yelled again with a grin.

All the other kids were laughing, and Wrigley noticed, looking at an apartment about 50 yards up on the right. Wrigley followed along but he wasn't quite sure why they were yelling about a guy named Putney Swope.

"What's going on?" he asked Biggs.

"Just be ready to run," Biggs told him. "We've been doing this for a long time. The guys never wanted to take you along. When they saw you coming I begged them to let you come this time. Don't worry, it's just a bit of fun."

Elliott, looking around and puffing on his smoke with squinty eyes, snuck up to a patio apartment. Inside, the TV was blaring an old black and white western.

"Putney Swope says you got to have...*oh shit!*" Elliott yelled, running back toward the gang.

Up over the fence came a six-foot man in his 40s dressed in a jogging suit.

"You little bastard!" the man yelled out. "I'm gonna kick your ass this time!"

"Run!" yelled Elliott, wheeling it, somehow managing to continue smoking. The regular puffs of smoke made him look like a speeding locomotive at dusk. Everyone ran right past Wrigley, who froze for a moment, until he saw the outline of the man in the jogging suit coming in his direction, and then he made a break for it. All the other kids were 20—some even 40—yards in front of Wrigley, but now they were turning to see if he was okay. The tall jogger was sprinting toward Wrigley and yelling, "You little creep!" The man easily pulled up next to Wrigley, and just as he was about to grab Wrigley by his collar, his face changed.

"Wait," he said, slowing up a step or two, and still managing to pace with Wrigley, who was chugging as fast as he could, "you're the blind kid."

Wrigley stopped in his tracks and glared at the jogger. The jogger looked at Wrigley, confused, taken aback by Wrigley's face, which morphed into a scowl. "I'm faster than *you*, old man!" And with that, Wrigley took off.

He saw everyone in the gang make a hard left into the Hong Kong Motel. They ran through a gate, across the pool area and hid in the bushes. Wrigley knew this motel well because he had cleaned the pool for a few years for spare cash. The jogger got over his confusion, took on a scowl of his own, and darted after Wrigley. "Get *back* here, four eyes!" He ran to within 15 feet of Wrigley, who made a hard left, sprinting through the Hong Kong Motel's heavy metal gate he saw his friends enter, holding it back like a slingshot with its big strong spring and letting go at the very last second. The jogger was reaching out to get his hands on Wrigley when the gate sprung back and hit him square in the face, knocking him over.

The jogger was out cold. "Guys?" Wrigley said cautiously, looking down at the jogger's unconscious body and swelling face. "*Guys!* Come out and help!"

Slowly, out of the bushes behind the motel pool came Biggs, Elliott, George, Black Patty, and Monty Jack. They formed a circle around the body.

"Whoa, Sandy," said Black Patty. "Cool move."

"I think," Wrigley said, breathing heavy, "I *killed* him."

"Nah," Elliott said, unmoved. "Seen plenty of dead guys." He reached down, put his hand on the jogger's neck and felt a pulse. "He's not dead."

The jogger suddenly reached up and grabbed Elliott by the throat. "Now I got you, you little bastard! You're not going to ruin my movies with your Putney bullshit again!"

Everyone stood in shock. Elliott gasped. He was turning blue. "Just…a…joke," he managed to squeak out. The jogger continued to clamp his hand around Elliott's throat.

"You're *choking* him!" Biggs exploded, stating the obvious.

"That I am," the jogger said with a low growl, his face red with anger, veins popping out of his neck, as he stood up slowly and stared at Elliott.

"Mister," Monty Jack pleaded, "we were just playing around. We didn't mean no harm."

Slam! Wrigley came out of the darkness swinging a two by four like a baseball bat and plunked the jogger on the back of the head. The jogger went down, blood pouring from his head. This time he really was out. Elliott's face quickly went from blue to red. He dropped to the ground on all fours and coughed up some blood. The lady from the second story of the motel yelled out, "I called the cops!"

"Thanks, retard," Elliott spit out to Wrigley, as he helped him up. "I owe you one."

The entire gang except for Wrigley took off.

"Hey, Sandy!" Elliott called out, looking back to find Wrigley checking the jogger's pulse, "let's go!"

"Putney Swope is alive," said Wrigley, catching up to Elliott who was waiting for him, "but he's gonna have a big ass headache." Elliott cracked a sinister smile, clapped Wrigley on the shoulder, and urged him to make a break for it.

★ ★ ★

"Twenty-seven years," Toothpick said, admiring the flickering black-and-white image of Nolan Ryan on the den wall.

"5,714 career strikeouts in 27 years. Nobody, and I mean nobody, in all the history of baseball even comes close to the number of strikeouts Ryan had. Ever wonder why?"

Toothpick noticed Wrigley was rubbing his hung over head.

"My guess is his heater," Wrigley said lethargically. "The man could throw 100 miles an hour, Toothpick."

"More importantly," said Toothpick, "using his large body for leverage, he could put that 100-mile-an-hour fastball *wherever he wanted.*"

Toothpick played the film over and over in slow motion, stopping it when he needed to emphasize a point, but noticing that Wrigley was preoccupied by whatever was going on in his aching skull. "Get up here!" said Toothpick. "Copy his leg kick."

Wrigley looked up, his elbows resting on his thighs and his fingers pressing his temples, giving Toothpick a look that said, "*Are you serious?*"

"*Dead serious*," said Toothpick's own look.

Wrigley made a labored attempt to stand and walked to the middle of the den. He brought his left leg up high and promptly fell backward. Suddenly embarrassed, he popped right back up, took a deep breath and picked the leg up again.

"You might want to use your other leg, since you're primarily a lefty," said Toothpick, not pleased to see Wrigley in such poor condition, but happy to see him endure. Toothpick froze the film, and Wrigley looked at Ryan's leg kicked high in the air and about ready to explode toward the catcher. "Now the beginning of his windup is slow but right at the apex—*boom!*"

"Watch how he goes into a second gear," Toothpick said, "and blasts right down toward the plate, leading with his hip. Do you understand what he's doing here? See how far he strides? It lets him release the ball that much closer to the plate, so his fastball seems even faster to the hitter. And the man had some strong legs, Wrigs. He would work out within 24 hours of his starts to keep his body strong, way before anybody ever thought about doing that."

Wrigley was again losing focus. "What?" he said, noticing Toothpick's look of disappointment.

"You're not listening," Toothpick said.

"I'm not feeling so hot," Wrigley said.

"Headache?" Toothpick replied in a tone insinuating he knew exactly what it was from.

"Duh," said Wrigley.

"I think it's time for Falco," Toothpick said.

Wrigley looked up at Toothpick, impatient for an explanation.

"Freddy Falcone," Toothpick said, indulging him. "We also call him 'The Falcon.' Some say he threw upward of 120 miles per hour."

"What?" Wrigley moaned.

"He failed to make it to the major leagues, Wrigs. Didn't have the control of his pitches—or his *life*. Even though he could throw harder than probably any other pitcher who ever played the game, he also walked a lot of hitters. He holds the record for most walks and most strikeouts per nine innings of any pro pitcher in baseball." Looking squarely at Wrigley, Toothpick emphasized, "In the history of the game!"

"I get the point," Wrigley said grouchily.

Toothpick leaned right up to Wrigley's face. "He was an alcoholic."

"I only had two drinks," Wrigley said, backing away, offended.

"That's two drinks too many for me," Toothpick said. "If you want to keep working together."

Wrigley looked up, a little desperate. Then he looked down, his face morphing from contempt to something that resembled shame.

"You know about my grandpa's drinking, don't you?" Wrigley asked.

"Yes, Wrigs. I knew him pretty well," said Toothpick. "It was truly a shame that he didn't end up a pitching coach in the show. He had the skills, the knowledge. I think he even had the drive, but when he was young and at the crossroads, he made a fatal mistake."

"Marilyn?" Wrigley asked, having heard about this from Bubbs.

"It wasn't her. In fact, from what he told me, she asked him why he wasn't sticking with baseball. No, he was afraid to chase his dream, Wrigley. Then he turned to drinking hoping that would make him feel better. I mean he got to coach, but he could have gone down as one of the best in the game."

"I get it," Wrigley said. "I have a promise to keep." He stared Toothpick right in the eyes and didn't look away.

"I'll stick with you if we visit Falco," said Toothpick.

"Cool," Wrigley said. "Thank you."

★ ★ ★

Two weeks later, Wrigley and Toothpick were in Brooklyn at the Southside Retirement Village visiting Freddy "Falco" Falcone, who sat in a chair in his room, half asleep. *This saggy old man threw a baseball at 120 miles per hour*, thought Wrigley, incredulously. He looked small, maybe five ten and 115 pounds. But Wrigley noticed he had long, slender hands—a lot like his.

"How is my favorite pitcher?" Toothpick asked Falco.

Falco looked at Toothpick, and in a stern voice said, "Stark, you still owe me five bucks. Pay up."

"I'm not Stark," Toothpick said, rolling his eyes. Then, turning to Wrigley, "Doug Stark was a teammate of Falco's. They'd made a bet one day that Falco couldn't throw a baseball through an outfield wall. Falco had warmed up, and stepping just 15 feet away from the wall, threw the first pitch clear through the wood."

"Oh," said Falco. "Well. Then *someone* needs to pay up. Who *are* ya?"

"It's me," said Toothpick, "Rudy."

Falco squinted and smiled, "Oh, Rudy. Yes, of course. Hello. How's your father?"

Toothpick ignored the question. "This here is Wrigley Sanders," Toothpick said motioning to Wrigley. "He's a lefty, like you, and he…"

"A *lefty?*" Falco said, inspecting Wrigley's left arm. He was intrigued.

"Yeah," said Toothpick, "and he wants to try out for the Bigs."

Falco rubbed his stubbly chin, his eyes cleared, and he looked at Wrigley, right in his eyes.

"I'm a lefty. I thrown the ball so hard that I once tore off a batter's ear. No shit. When I thrown to Ted Williams, he wouldn't go back in the box. I think 'cause he shit his pants. I thrown the ball upwards of 120 miles an hour. Fact, one day back in Stockton, I broke umpire Harvey's mask in three places. Knocked him back 15 feet—and he's a big one."

Falco stopped and took a long, whistled breath. "But what I've never done, and *wish* I done," he said, now looking forlornly out the window, "is pitch in the majors."

Wrigley noticed Falco's eyes getting watery. "Um, Mr. Falco, sir," said Wrigley, interrupting Falco's reverie, "Toothpick here says you could help me. Give me some advice."

Falco looked back at Wrigley, his eyes getting big. "Toothpick?" he said, "where's Toothpick?"

Wrigley looked back at Toothpick, confused.

"The boy could really use your help," Toothpick said to Falco. "You're a lefty, he's a lefty…"

Falco held up his hand indicating for Toothpick to stop talking. He paused for a long while, looking for the sincerity behind the Coke-bottle glasses. It didn't take him long to find it. He scratched his chin, nodded his head, and held up a bony index finger each time he called out a number. "One: stay away from the sauce. It don't pay…it'll mess up your head. Two: listen to your coach. He may not be the sharpest pencil in the can, but if you listen, you'll be better off. I mean *really* listen, son! Three: don't yell at your teammates. They're on your side. Get plenty of sleep. Don't pick no artichokes—it's rough on your hands. And be a pitcher. That means first pitch strikes—lots of strikes." Then Falco, like some kind of battery-powered toy, gradually lost his steam, sat back in his chair, and smiled. "All I got."

"Amen," said Toothpick. He looked at Wrigley, who was still nodding his head, not really sure what this all meant, but feeling the weight of some sort of authority.

"Now," said Falco, "if you'll excuse me—Rudy, Wrigley—I'm expecting supper." Then, looking at Toothpick, he whispered excitedly, "They're serving Jell-O for dessert. Say 'hi' to your father."

"Thanks, Falco," said Toothpick, who nudged Wrigley toward the door.

Wrigley got the hint. "Thanks, Mr. Falco. No artichokes, I promise."

CHAPTER 14

I have to go lefty, Wrigley thought. *I go righty, Ruth parks it.* Wrigley took the sign, closed his eyes, listened to some inspirational self-talk, and threw all the pitches that were asked of him. Each time, his left elbow hurt more. Then he got to the critical pitch—the one that Charlie Root threw, that Ruth hit out. Just before he wound up for the final payoff pitch, his left arm went into a major spasm. Wrigley grabbed it and doubled over in pain. Toothpick ran out to the mound, the trainer fast on his heels.

Toothpick put his arm on a hunched over Wrigley, "Wrigs! What's going on, son?"

"Here, let me take a look at that," the trainer said calmly, seeing that Toothpick was becoming emotional. He examined Wrigley's left arm. Wrigley flinched in pain. "It's reinjured," said the trainer to Toothpick.

"Thanks for that," said Wrigley sarcastically.

"Throw another pitch or two and it could be your last with this arm," said the trainer, massaging Wrigley's arm. Wrigley regretted his reaction and looked up at the trainer with conflicted eyes. "I'm serious," said the trainer, conjuring up a more comforting tone. "Career ending."

★ ★ ★

"What do I do?" Wrigley asked Biggs, standing in Bubbs' den, looking down at the old lady fast asleep. "She invited me over to watch the game, but she looks really out." Biggs gave Wrigley a sideways glance. "More than usual," added Wrigley.

"She must've had a late night," Biggs said, shrugging his shoulders. "She doesn't always sleep."

The speakers in the Santino family den purred with the voice of Vin Scully. Biggs and Wrigley were about to walk out of the room when Bubbs woke up and practically screamed, "Sandy's perfect game! Sit down!"

"She likes to listen to this," Biggs said to Wrigley. "It's the last three outs of Sandy K's game in '65."

"September 9," Bubbs suddenly said. "Pisssssh. Listen."

Vin Scully's voice, smooth and comforting, was in the middle of describing the last inning of action. "I would think that the mound in Dodger Stadium right now is the loneliest place in the world. Sandy, fussing, looks in to get his sign. Oh and two to Amalfitano. The strike-two pitch to Joe, fastball swung on and missed—strike three. He is one out away from the Promised Land!"

"It's against the Cubs!" Wrigley said to no one in particular.

"Sssssshhhh!" Bubbs whispered, putting her fingers to her lips, giving Wrigley a reprimanding look. "*Listen!*"

"She's memorized the whole game," Biggs whispered.

"Shut up!" Bubbs said, violently gesturing to him a *simmer down*. "Here comes another strike out. That curve goes all the way from twelve o'clock to six o'clock. He ends up striking out the last 6 batters. *Nobody* does that! Nobody. Listen."

"Now Sandy looks in, in to his windup, the two-one pitch to Kueen. Swung on and missed; strike two. It is 9:46 p.m. Two and two to Harvey Kueen. One strike away. Sandy into his windup; here's the pitch. Swung on and missed. The perfect game!"

"Hear that?!" Bubbs said. "Listen to the fans cheer. Vinny doesn't talk over them for over 30 seconds. He knows this is about the fans. A perfect game."

All three of them listened to the cheering of the crowd, then finally, Vinny came back in: "On the scoreboard in right field, it is 9:46 p.m. In the City of the Angels, Los Angeles, California. And the crowd of 29,139 just sitting in to see the only pitcher in baseball history to hurl four no-hit, no-run games. He's done it four straight years, and now he's capped it. On his fourth no-hitter, he made it a perfect game."

Wrigley felt a chill blast down his spine. Bubbs, nearly in tears, said, "Sometimes I listen to this game, and I'm afraid somebody is gonna get a hit." Biggs and Wrigley smiled at each other.

"Fourteen strikeouts," Bubbs went on, "Santo, Banks, Williams—those guys couldn't *touch* him." Biggs mouthed the names of the players behind Bubbs' back as she listed them. He motioned for Wrigley to sit down. "I'll check back," he said, leaving the room.

Wrigley sat down, not sure what to say as Bubbs continued to happily stare into space.

"Wrigs," she said looking around, "Wrigs!"

"Right here!" Wrigley said waving from the couch.

Bubbs looked at him and smiled. "Good you're sitting. You want to learn how to pitch?"

"Yes, ma'am," he said, afraid to answer anything else.

"You know, Sandy K didn't start out being the ace of the team," Bubbs said. "In fact, for his first five years, he was a mess. Didn't have a curveball. Tried to throw the ball through the backstop every pitch. Then Sherry told him to dial it all back."

"*Norm* Sherry?" Wrigley said, proud to know the reference.

"Of course, smart ass, who else?" Bubbs said, not pleased by the interruption. "Anyway, this second-string catcher tells Sandy to dial it back, and…"

"He did better?" Wrigley interrupted again.

Bubbs looked at Wrigley like he'd better not try that again. "*That's* the understatement of the century. When Sandy listened to Norm, and most pitchers with their big egos wouldn't have, his fastball didn't lose any velocity. It started to look like it was rising about a foot. You put together a rising fastball and a curve like Sandy threw, and you get magic. Sometimes, taking the foot off the pedal gives you more heat."

"I can throw that pitch," Wrigley casually said without thinking about the ramifications of claiming that to Bubbs.

Bubbs looked at Wrigley dead in the eyes, and stressing each syllable added, "Oh you can, huh? How many times? Sandy threw one hundred forty, sometimes *a hundred sixty*, pitches. He was strong, like an ox. Even today, he has back muscles of a mule. Wrigley?"

"Yes, ma'am?"

"Don't let those newfangled pitching coaches baby you, son."

"Yes, ma'am!" Wrigley said as Biggs ducked his head back into the room.

"Time to go," Biggs said with a grin. "There's talk of heading to the Kern River."

Wrigley looked at Bubbs, his face inquiring whether he was excused.

"Go on, Wrigs," Bubbs said sitting back in her chair and offering a smile of approval.

Wrigley smiled and turned to leave.

"Wrigs!" called out Bubbs. Wrigley turned around quickly and sprung to attention.

"Show me a guy who can't pitch inside, and I'll show you a *loser*," she said earnestly. Then, breaking in to a smile, she said, "Now get out of here!"

Wrigley nodded and followed Biggs out of the den.

"Koufax?" Biggs asked.

"Koufax."

"Thought so."

★ ★ ★

He knew he should have been packing for Kern River, because they were leaving in the morning, but Wrigley spent most of the night looking at Koufax footage. He wanted some of that control, pitching to the inside part of the plate. And that power! He wanted to feel that power. Maybe he'd take his foot off the gas a little during his next pitching session and see how that worked. He listened to the whole perfect game he'd gotten from his neighbor Tom Smith. The combination of Koufax's genius on the mound and Vin Scully's poetry from the booth was magic. Afterward, he'd never felt so fired up.

From the car, they all saw the sign posted right at the entrance of town stating how many people had drowned in the Kern River so far this year. It read, "26."

"That must be a mistake," Biggs said as they drove past the sign.

"Never seen a number that big," said Hoe.

Within minutes they arrived at camp, a dusty barren area next to the river. Immediately, everyone was out of their cars and claiming tent sites. And within five minutes, Wrigley came tumbling out of a tent, with his arms locked around Elliott's head.

"Son of bitch tried to take my spot," Elliott yelled.

"Lies!" said Wrigley, brown dust puffing out of his mouth, his glasses fogged, crooked and slipping off his nose from the sweat on his face.

Everyone calmly continued to stake in their tents, with Biggs, George, Hoe, Black Patty, and Monty Jack all rolling their eyes.

"I swear to god I'll kill you!" Elliott yelled once he escaped the headlock and stood across from Wrigley, who was trying to adjust his glasses to get ready for the next round.

"Let's cool it guys," Biggs said, bored. "It's time to eat."

Monty Jack put on the boom box. *"And another one gone, and another one gone, and other one bites the dust."* Everyone slowly gathered around a few wood picnic tables. George, Black Patty, and Monty Jack all had funny smirks on their faces. Two bowls of tuna salad sat in the middle of the table along with a loaf of bread. George handed the smaller bowl to Wrigley along with a piece of bread.

"Thanks," Wrigley said.

"Sure," George replied. Then he whispered in Elliott's direction, "Cat food."

Elliott sat up with a grin and whispered, "What do ya say? Fun?"

Wrigley smelled the cat food, "Yum! I like mine with more mayo!"

A few giggles broke the silence as Wrigley generously applied mayo to his cat food.

He took a bite (while the whole table held their breath), licked his lips, and said, "My mom makes it with white tuna and relish, but this dark stuff tastes good too."

The whole table burst into laughter. Elliott, sensing an opening, bolted back to the tent, grabbed Wrigley's duffle bag, and sprinted down toward the water.

"Hey?" Wrigley said, suddenly alarmed. "Hey!" Wrigley quickly gave chase, but Elliott got to the water first, opened Wrigley's duffle bag, and tossed it into the rapids.

Wrigley took one look at his stuff floating down the river and instinctively gave chase. He stripped off his shoes and socks, took off his glasses, *gently* putting them into one of his shoes, then pulled his t-shirt violently over his head and tossed it aside.

He was about to jump in when he looked around like he forgot something, turned to Elliott, ran over to him, and blasted him in the gut with a left hook. Elliott collapsed on to the ground gasping for air. Wrigley smiled and nodded, then returned to the task of retrieving his gear and jumped in the river. The other fellas weren't even paying attention. Since Wrigley learned how to give what he got from Elliott, it had been years since they felt the need to come to his defense. Elliott's and Wrigley's antics had become just a part of the scenery.

Wrigley hit the water and swam with all his might. He saw his mitt a few inches under the surface and tried to grab it. But within seconds, his arms and legs felt like over-cooked spaghetti. The water was cold, so cold his testicles snapped up inside his body. His left calf began to spasm then cramp up into a rock-hard softball sized muscle bursting against his tight skin—his mitt slowly floated out of sight.

Wrigley was losing gas and started to go down. Blue-green water rushed past his face in a blur. He kicked with one leg and dog-paddled with his weighted-down, frozen arms. His feet touched the bottom for a moment. He let out a couple of bubbles of air, hoping it would relieve the pain in his lungs. He gulped a few bites of water and closed his eyes. His body went limp. It was dark, cold. On his left, he saw a bright, dime-sized light. He turned to it. There was a huge roar and flash.

★ ★ ★

He smelled peanuts first, then sweat. His surroundings slowly coming into focus, he realized he was inside the Cubs locker room, getting dressed, putting on a baseball uniform. His name was on the locker in big black letters. **SANDERS**. He started to button his top and saw a flash of bright color off to his left. He looked at his reflection in a giant mirror and saw a huge Cubs logo, in full red, white, and blue, tattooed on the whole left side of his body and wrapping around his back.

He looked down and smiled at the giant logo. *Cool*, he thought. He finished dressing, looked around the empty locker room, and walked toward the field, through a dark tunnel into the brightness. The stands were packed. Men wore derbies and pinstriped suits. He saw a few women in bonnets. Everyone was dressed up. He looked over to the dugout and noticed his teammates—he intuited they were his teammates—each wearing the grey and black Cubs baseball cap with a black C and black brim Wrigley recognized as the 1908 away hat. He took his hat off and stared at it, a black and grey thing of beauty.

★ ★ ★

Biggs looked back toward the river and saw only Elliott. He got a sinking feeling in his stomach and walked over. "Elliott," he said suspiciously, "where *is* he?"

Elliott was searching the water with his eyes, concerned. "The retard decided to go swimming," he said, worry in his voice.

"Another one bites the dust…"

Biggs' eyes got big, terrified. *"Guys!"* he screamed.

All talk stopped, everyone looked over at Biggs. "He's in the river!" Biggs yelled.

★ ★ ★ ⋆

Standing on the field at the gate of the bullpen, dressed in his 1908 Cubs uniform, Wrigley took in the sold-out crowd. Everyone seemed to be looking at him. He looked at the mound, took a deep breath, and took his first step to the mound, excited that he was about to finally pitch for the Cubs. Then everything went black.

★ ★ ★ ⋆

"I got him!" Biggs yelled, "I got him!" Biggs yanked on Wrigley's legs, ripping him up from the water. Fleck, strong blond-haired and muscular, along with Hoe, helped drag Wrigley to the shore and put him on his back. Wrigley's body was whiter than a home team uniform on opening day. His face was grey as the visitors' hats, and the rings under his eyes looked like eye black—the grease ballplayers use to diminish sun glare.

"Does anyone know CPR?" Biggs said desperately.

Elliott, shaking, knelt down by Wrigley's body and unconsciously pushed Biggs aside. "I do," he said. "Sort of…"

Elliott pancaked his right palm over the back of his left hand, interlaced his fingers, placed his stacked hands and straight arms over Wrigley's chest, and started pumping. "1, 2, 3,…" he exhaled sharply with each compression.

"C'mon retard…" he said desperately, when suddenly, water and some air blasted out of Wrigley's mouth.

"No," Wrigley seemed to say while gasping for air. Then after a big breath, he let out a clear and adamant, "*No!*"

The color slowly returned to Wrigley's face, he looked up at his friends, horrified. He sat up, looked around at nothing in particular and said, "Oh shit, really?" Then, pushing himself up by his hands to a confident standing position, "I've gotta go."

Wrigley walked away from the Lasaine Gang with a determined stride toward his tent. The gang stayed where they were, frozen, stunned, like they had seen a ghost.

They still weren't sure they hadn't as they watched Wrigley methodically roll up his sleeping bag, fold up the tent, place everything in his duffle bag, and start down the trail that led to the main highway. He paused, turned, walked back to his shoes, took his glasses, carefully placed them on his face and, leaving his socks, shirt, and shoes behind turned back, and walked back toward the trail.

"What about your glove?" Biggs yelled out.

Wrigley just waved his hand and kept on walking, not saying a word.

Three hours later, after Biggs and Fleck decided they'd had enough and wanted to head home, they found Wrigley sitting roadside with a bad sunburn, rocking back and forth, tossing a rock back and forth into his bare, bloody hands.

"What the hell is he doing?" Fleck said.

Fleck pulled up near Wrigley, and Biggs rolled down the passenger-seat window. "Wrigs!" he said, "jump in!"

"No thanks," Wrigley replied, unperturbed as he continued to play with the rock.

"Come on," Biggs whined, "it's going to be dark in a few hours. You know how cold it gets in the Mojave."

"I lost my mitt," Wrigley said plainly. "From now on, I take care of myself."

"Oh shit," Biggs whispered to Fleck. "I gotta go get him."

"He looks a little weird," Fleck whispered, "be careful."

Biggs shot Fleck a disapproving look and then got out of the car. Wrigley didn't even turn his head toward him when he heard the crunch of the gravel on the roadside. Biggs paused for a moment then reached his arm down to give Wrigley a lift up. Wrigley continued to ignore him.

"Come on," Biggs said, folding his arms.

Wrigley appeared to concede, as he grabbed Biggs' arm with his bloody hands, pulled him down to the ground so quickly he knocked the air out of Biggs. Wrigley climbed on top of Biggs and put his forearm firmly against his throat, putting pressure on his stunned friend's Adam's apple.

"Leave. Me. Alone." Wrigley said slowly, ominously. "I was perfectly fine in the river. I was a Cub. I was a pitcher. I was THERE. At Wrigley…"

Biggs saw his eyes were vacant. "Wrigs," he said calmly, "it's me. Biggs."

Wrigley, blinking his eyes rapidly, shook his head so hard that his glasses fell off. Straddling his friend, he looked down at his bloody hands and back to Biggs.

He suddenly took on a look of horror and rolled off Biggs, sitting next to him, confused. He started to sob.

"I was a Cub," Wrigley said through his tears. "I was a Cub…"

Biggs lay there on the ground staring up at the sky, catching his breath. Finally, Fleck came out, taking in the scene, not sure what to say, when he heard George.

"Guys!" George yelled out from a distance, "Guys!" Suddenly he was upon them, hands on his knees, catching his breath. He looked up, smiling. "Guys," he said more calmly, "look what *I* found." Wrigley's glove was in his left hand.

★ ★ ★

"He said 'career ending,' right? We should pull you right now," Toothpick said to Wrigley, looking for the manager, who arrived seconds later on the mound, along with the umpire.

"What do we have here?" the manager asked.

"I'm fine," Wrigley said, holding his left arm like a dead snake. "I just needed a breather. I'll go with my right."

They all looked at each other as if to ask, "Is this guy serious?"

"Make your call, Coach," said the umpire. "It's time to play ball."

Toothpick gestured for the manager, trainer, and umpire to leave the mound. The manager was reluctant, but remembered he'd have no choice but to go to Gonzalez, who was not exactly the person he'd want in this jam.

"You really want to do this?" Toothpick asked.

"Once in a lifetime, right, Toothpick?" Wrigley said, looking up at him and smiling as he gazed to the skies. "It's Cubs' baseball. Anything can happen."

Toothpick smiled, thinking how many times he'd heard Connor Kelly say that, and shook his head and jogged off. Wrigley waved to Connor, signifying he was ready to go.

Connor went through the signals until Wrigley nodded "yes." Then Wrigley looked right into the eyes of Ruth and gave him a huge crooked-toothed smile, his ragged teeth sparkling in the stadium lighting. Ruth, seeing Wrigley's crooked yet razor-sharp teeth, wondered what the heck this bushy-headed four-eyed man was thinking.

Wrigley went into his left-handed windup. But instead of throwing a high fastball like Charlie Root did, he tossed a perfectly placed knuckleball, pushing it toward Ruth, high and inside. At the end of his release, Wrigley heard something pop in his arm but the ball continued to move through the air, traveling at half the speed of his fastball.

Babe Ruth, known to have been able to pick up the spin of a ball within six feet of its release, looked at this ball and was confounded. It didn't have any spin, coming at him with the seams stuck turned up, like a wicked smile.

Ruth didn't want anything to do with this ball, but it seemed to have eyes—for his head. He'd duck back, and the ball would follow; he'd move over the plate, and the ball would jig over the plate. In the last ten feet, the ball went right for Ruth's face. He jerked away from the plate as the ball zipped back over it.

"Strike three!" yelled the umpire.

★ ★ ★

Wrigley took a full week off after his river incident, watching his favorite films of old-time pitchers and oiling his mitt. He also spent time memorizing Vin Scully's call of the last three outs of Koufax's perfect game. The first time he worked with Toothpick using his "Vinny Voice" and announcing to himself, Toothpick noticed Wrigley throwing some of his best pitches ever. Wrigley felt he was getting a sense of the Koufax power and was now looking for a way to get that same kind of control with his Overall drop ball. He decided it was time to pay his neighbor Tom a visit.

Thomas "Wingfoot" Smith was a 70-something-year-old poet, inventor, and out-of-work movie soundman, skinny as a wire with unruly, long, grey hair and a salt-and-pepper speckled beard that seemed to be in a state of perpetual motion. During the gas shortage, he siphoned gas from people's cars, and when he was caught, said he needed a gallon to take his wife to the doctor. His pathetic appearance allowed him to sell the story more often than was reasonable. He designed and built a custom 18-hole putt-putt golf course, complete with windmill and pond—in his backyard. He would gaze at the stars and predict earthquakes on a nightly basis, and when the big one hit, which it did every decade or two, would stand on his barren front yard and crow to the sky about how he had, "Preee-dicted it. Yessirreeeeee." Tom would do handstands in a clown outfit and play his harmonica for giggles.

One day, when Wrigley was eight or nine, he wandered by Tom's place—located on the block between Hoe and

George—and, through blurry vision, Wrigley saw Tom toiling with what looked like a glider of some sort.

"Young man!" Tom called out to a nearly blind Wrigley, "You a pilot?"

"Nope!" called out Wrigley. "I'm a *pitcher!*"

"Close enough," said Tom with a nod, "C'mon over here!"

Wrigley moved toward the glider and noticed that Tom, with a somewhat wild look in his eyes, seemed to be a hurricane of energy. Wrigley felt hypnotized, afraid something bad might happen but also excited that perhaps, just perhaps, he would be able to fly! With Wrigley's help, Tom hustled his flying machine, a small, hand-built glider, into the back of his old red '65 Ford pickup truck.

"Ain't she a beaut?" Tom said, as Wrigley stopped near the passenger door and stared at what used to be a spiffy white hood—it now had paint flaking off to the bare metal.

"Hop in!" he said to Wrigley, opening the passenger door and gesturing to the seat. Like a cautious parent, Tom carefully strapped Wrigley in with a seat beat. "Comfy?" asked Tom.

"Y…y…yeah," said Wrigley, not sure what was happening but anxious to find out. The truck sputtered down the road to the local corn patch.

"Ready?" Tom said over the noise of the truck.

"Yeah?" Wrigley said, shrugging his shoulders, unable to conceal a smile, but not really knowing *what* he was ready for.

"Good enough," said Tom, slowing down and getting out of the truck. "Let's go."

Tying a rope to the front of the plane and the back of the truck, Tom carefully strapped in young Wrigley into the contraption using an old seat belt he'd installed just for this purpose. His hands were so excited they shook, and it took him three tries to click the latch.

"Hang on kid. You'll be in airborne in no time," Tom said, his skinny body trembling as he ran back toward the truck.

"This thing have any controls?" Wrigley asked looking at the bare front dashboard of the glider.

"Nope," Tom called out. "Just hold on, I'll drive and it'll lift off the ground and glide around in circles. It'll be on automatic pilot."

"But how do I land?"

"Softly, once she loses her altitude," returned Tom.

"Okay," Wrigley said, his own body now starting to tremble. Tom wet his finger and tried to find which direction the wind was blowing. The thing was, it really wasn't blowing much.

Unsatisfied, Tom jumped in his truck and revved the engine, then popped the clutch and stomped his accelerator to the floor. The old Ford rumbled over the corn patch, the rope went taut and Wrigley and the plane skidded and ripped a pretty good-sized furrow in the soft ground of the cornfield.

Wrigley was having the time of his life. He didn't know if he was on the ground or off the ground—the glider never really came up off the ground more than a foot or two—all he knew was he was flying, fast and furious. He felt like he was fired out of a Jules Verne cannon, right through Shoeless Joe's cornfield. The stories Papa read to him had come to life!

Tom slowed the truck down until he came to a stop. He shut off the engine, threw open the door, and ran back to find his flying machine with both wings torn. The bottom was scratched up something awful. Inside, sat a cackling, smiling Wrigley. For Tom, the sight of young Wrigley's smile alleviated the horror of seeing his wrecked machine.

"Sorry couldn't get that thing more in the air," Tom said, putting a hand on the top of Wrigley's head. "Maybe next time?"

Wrigley just stared at his new friend wide-eyed, with a plastered smile. It was the most fun he'd ever had.

★ ★ ★

"Tom?" the now grown-up Wrigley yelled through his neighbor's front screen door. "Tom, you home?"

"Come on in!" responded Tom. Wrigley opened the door and peered inside, glancing around to make sure there weren't any contraptions to trip him up. Tom wasn't a conscious prankster, but it was clear from his scrapes, scars, and on a couple occasions, singed scalp, that *his inventions* were playing pranks on *him*—and potentially unsuspecting guests. In addition to metal scraps, wood shards, and hubcaps, Tom's house was filled with old food, empty bottles of beer, and overflowing trash cans that combined to put out a stench that hit Wrigley in the face like the stinging fog of a mother skunk protecting her young. Wrigley weathered the storm as he entered the kitchen to find Tom at the counter enhancing, fixing, or dismantling what looked to be a milkshake maker.

"Tom," Wrigley said, "I need some help with a physics issue."

"Well! Look who's here," said Tom putting down the screwdriver and taking off his protective goggles, "Wrigs, good to see ya. You've come to the right place. Tell me a little more!"

"Well," Wrigley said. "I'm trying out for the college baseball team. I need to analyze a pitching motion. I'm trying to pitch like the great ones—you know, Koufax, Ryan, Marichal."

"Did you say '*Marichal*'?" Tom said, distastefully, like he had just beheld the redolence of his house. "He was a Giant."

"But…he could…"

"I know, I know," Tom conceded. "He *was* pretty good. I get it."

Wrigley went on, "I study their movement on film, but sometimes I just don't get the results I want. Right now, I'm trying to perfect Orval Overall's drop ball. I'm missing something. A movement or…I don't know."

"Orval who?" Tom asked.

"*Overall*," Wrigley responded, adding, "a Cub, *not* a Giant."

Tom nodded and smiled. "Do you have any pictures or film of this guy?"

"Black-and-white film on Super-8."

"Good, good," Tom said nodding. "Bring it to me, and let's see what I can come up with. Perhaps wire drawings will help you."

Wrigley looked at him quizzically.

"Never mind," he said, "bring me the film tomorrow, and we'll sort out this drop ball overalls issue. I'll be in the field testing out some magic beans, so leave it in the mailbox and come back in 72 hours."

Three days later, Wrigley returned, and this time when he entered the house, the living room had a large clearing in the middle. The dining room table was spotless.

A week's worth of dishes and old food were replaced with wires, cables, a few rolls of white trainer's tape. On the far end of the room sat a projector and screen.

"Sit down, kid," Tom said, "and take off your shirt."

Tom quickly put small sensors onto Wrigley's body with the trainer tape. He went from the tip of his hands to his shoulders, down his torso, all the way to the tips of his toes, connecting small bits of wire along the way every foot or so. He connected all the wires to a small device.

"What's all the wire for?" Wrigley asked.

"You'll see," he said as he turned down the lights. "Now, watch the screen."

"That's Overall!" Wrigley said.

"Yup," Tom said, "Now watch this—and watch *carefully*."

As Orval wound up, all of his limbs and his torso were highlighted in florescent green while the rest of his image became soft, almost hard to see. It looked like a Halloween skeleton costume in the dark, except you could really see how the body moved because of the stick-figure image.

"Whoa, that's cool!" Wrigley said.

"Yup," Tom said. "I'm gonna put it in slow motion now. Orval was a pretty big man. Watch how he rocked back, putting all his weight onto his back leg, with his left leg acting like a fulcrum."

"Never noticed that before…" Wrigley said, still entranced.

"Now you stand up," Tom said excitedly. "I'm gonna turn this black light onto you and film *you*."

Wrigley snapped out of it. "Excuse me?"

"I want you to do your best imitation of Orval's windup," Tom said. "Up, up!"

Tom turned on a black light, and next, the camera. In the darkness, all you could see was the fluorescent green stick figure of Wrigley doing his Orval windup.

"Good," Tom said, "Now, wait here." He ran off into the other room. Wrigley heard some rustling, and a couple minutes later, Tom was back. He turned on the lights, set up the camera, turned the lights back down, and said, "Watch." He played both of the projectors at the same time, starting one, then the other, and overlaying the stick figure of Wrigley right over the top of Orval.

Wrigley stood in shock and amazement, as his leg, then Orval's leg, raised up to the sky simultaneously. His angle was a little different, his speed was off just a tad, but what he noticed most was when Orval came toward the plate, his hip, unlike Wrigley's, was way ahead of the rest of his body.

"Do you see any little differences?" Tom said.

"Lead with my hips," said Wrigley smiling. "My hips. Toothpick told me to lead with my hips. Orval does that. So does Nolan Ryan."

It took a few weeks working with Tom but soon he was moving in unison with Orval and figured out how to throw his famous "dropper" pitch to a T. Now the ball would go toward home plate, then at the last instant, just drop, almost straight down, hitting the backside of the plate—a pitch that would be nearly impossible to hit.

CHAPTER 15

The crowd went nuts after Ruth struck out and angrily walked off the field. Wrigley felt like he was starting to own this time warp. He couldn't explain what was going on, but his body tingled with the excitement he had felt at the bottom of the Kern River so long ago.

Wrigley caught the ball back from Connor, whose face he could make out behind the mask, and it was smiling. "Two down, Wrigs!"

"One more," Wrigley said to himself, as he walked back to the mound. He rubbed the ball with his hands when he heard the voice of announcer Pat Pieper, the legendary Cubs P.A. man.

"Ladies and gentlemen," said the gravelly voice, "now batting: the Iron Horse. Lou Gehrig."

"Oh no," Wrigley whispered

Wrigley knew Gehrig had hit a home run right after Ruth's called shot to cap off the World Series game three against the Cubs back on October 1, 1932. *Not this time*, thought Wrigley.

He held the runner on first, throwing back once to keep him honest. Was that Frank Chance playing first? Wrigley rubbed his eyes, but sure enough, there he was, the first baseman and manager of the Cubbies, in full pinstripe regalia. If only Bubbs could see him now!

Wrigley focused on Gehrig and watched him take a few beautiful practice swings. He didn't have any holes or weak spots. But Wrigley had also watched film on Lou and knew he'd hit a low fastball over the right field bleachers for his home run against Root.

Wrigley toed the rubber and turned to see if a pitcher was standing up. He was hoping and praying for a right-hander because his left elbow was starting to swell. In the distance, a big fair-haired figure slowly rose in the stands. Wrigley did a double take.

It was right-hander Johnny Kucks. Wrigley knew Johnny's pitches because he had watched a film of him throw a complete game shutout in the 1956 World Series against the Dodgers—as a Yankee. He loved how Johnny's ball gradually sunk low to force most batters to hit grounders. Wrigley wasn't sure why a Yankee was standing up to volunteer to pitch against his own team, but his gut told him to trust it.

★ ★ ★

"I'm off to tryouts Mom," Wrigley said, dressed in full 1908 Cubbie gear, walking out the door.

"Good luck, Wrigs!" she called back. "You can do it!"

"Betsy is all ready," Biggs said when Wrigley jumped in to Biggs' classic 1978 brown "woody" Pontiac Grand Safari. "Been tightening her up all week."

They pulled out of Wrigley's driveway past the palm trees that grew over two hundred feet into the blue, warm skies of Van Nuys past Wrigley's junior high, past his high school, past Balboa Park where they'd played so much baseball over the years.

"Been a wild ride, huh, Wrigs?" Biggs finally said, watching Wrigley look at his childhood ballfields pass by.

"Yep," Wrigley said as he pulled off his baseball shoes and put his stockinged feet up on the windshield. They drove on the Ventura Freeway, turned on to Malibu Canyon - a still undeveloped jewel of a road with rolling green hills - a creek, and a beautiful albeit small canyon—the same canyon where Annie rode her horse as a young woman. They blasted through the final tunnel, and the ocean air hit them, cool and foggy. The temperature dropped a good 20 degrees. Betsy was moving right along at 40 miles an hour, maybe 50.

"Oh boy," Biggs said.

"What?"

"Um," Biggs said, trying to sound casual, "we may have a brake problem."

"Not biting," Wrigley said with a smile.

"I must've left the plug out of the break line," Biggs said as he pumped the breaks to show Wrigley. "Nothing."

"What if you just down shift?" asked Wrigley, "That'll do the trick, right?"

Biggs looked at Wrigley and shrugged. "Worth a shot," he said, then took the column shifter in his right hand and gently downshifted.

"What the fuuuuu…" Biggs said, holding up the shifter, which had broken off.

They both looked ahead at the same time and saw a stoplight at the bottom of the hill, about five hundred yards away. Behind the light were at least 20 cars, all lined up waiting for the light to turn. Betsy was closing the gap fast.

"Slam her into the wall," Wrigley said. "It'll slow her down."

"No," Biggs said. "Can't do that."

"I will!" Wrigley said.

"Don't you dare," Biggs said. But it was too late. Wrigley opened up the passenger door and held it against the dirt cliff just outside. Biggs winced as the scrapping sound became louder and louder.

"No!" screamed Biggs, "The wood!"

"It's fake!" Wrigley said.

"Ah crap!" Biggs yelled back, realizing he had to concede. "Fine, close it!"

Wrigley closed the door. Biggs looked in the rear view, his side view mirror, then pulled the big, bright, highly waxed classic Pontiac Grand Safari away from the dirt cliff, quickly turned the wheel to the right, and slammed his pride and joy hard into the steep wall.

"That didn't help," Biggs said, the wagon still moving along.

"Again!" Wrigley said.

Biggs repeated the process, and while the second smash slowed them down a bit, they only had three hundred yards between them and the cars.

"The church has an uphill driveway, right?" asked Wrigley. "A big parking lot that we can circle until we stop?"

"Yes, yes!" Biggs said, excited.

They were about one hundred yards out from the church entrance, and everything started to slow down. They came up to the driveway. It did have a good 30 degree slant. The big wagon hit the cement going about 40. It flew through the air and landed without slowing down a bit.

"Whoooooooooaaaaaaaaaaaaaa, Betsy!" Biggs yelled.

They landed and started to turn; the tires screeched and smoked. Through the smoke, Wrigley saw about 20 Catholic girls in their grey-and-white checkered dresses, white socks, and shiny black shoes, playing hopscotch right in the parking lot.

"Mother Mary," Wrigley moaned.

In the group stood a pasty-skinned nun with wire-rimmed glasses and short-cut grey hair. She had a sharp beak of a nose and close-set eyes. She was frantically waving to her kids and yelling "Get out, get out, *now!*"

"Hold on!" Biggs said. Wrigley braced himself but his stockinged feet were pressing right on the bottom of his baseball shoes on the floor. Suddenly, Biggs turned the wheel sharply to the right, missing the kids and giving him a choice of flying off a cliff to certain death or smashing directly into a parked school bus, which he did, with an enormous BANG! The bus moved a full foot from the blow, with the whole front end of the wagon having instantly crumbled like a squeezebox. Steam blasted through the shattered windshield. Wrigley's feet were cut up and bleeding from pressing on his baseball cleats, his face cut from the shattered glass. Biggs looked to his left, rolled down his window, and the sharp-beaked nun was in his face, her cheeks swollen with red capillaries ready to burst.

"You son of a bitch!" the nun spat through clenched teeth. "You could've killed my kids! You son…son of a…"

Suddenly, a strong, uniformed arm came in and around the nun's waist. "It's okay sister," the cop said. "These boys did the best they could. I'm bettin' they lost their brakes. Could have been a whole lot worse. Lucky they kept their cool…"

The nun, shocked, turned to him, looked at the offending hand and shook it off violently. She shot nasty looks between the cop and the pale white passengers, and stomped back to her flock.

"Thanks, officer," Biggs said.

"You boys hear the sirens?" the officer asked.

"Nope," Biggs said. Wrigley had been silently picking the bits of glass out of his face and wiping down his neck. Suddenly he opened his door and said, "That's it. I gotta go. I can't be late."

"You're kiddin' me," Biggs said. "Look at your feet."

"Not missing my tryout!" Wrigley said, trying to put his baseball shoes on over his bloody feet and putting his 1908 Cubs hat over his blood-speckled head.

"You're a Cubs fan?" the cop said, noticing Wrigley's hat.

"All my life," Wrigley said.

"Me too," the cop said. "Where's the tryout?"

"Pepperdine," Wrigley said.

"Get in, Cubbie! I'll get you there," the cop said with wry grin.

Minutes later, Wrigley came blasting onto the Pepperdine campus with full sirens blaring, with the cop screeching to a stop right near the baseball diamond. Everyone on the field froze. One guy put his hands up in jest!

Coach Barnes, a big bull of a man who looked more like a linebacker than a baseball player, walked over to the car—his look betraying more offense rather than concern over a cop car doing its best imitation of the General Lee.

"What's seems to be the problem, officer?" demanded Barnes.

The cop sarcastically gestured to Wrigley like he was a night-show host presenting a guest. Barnes took one look at Wrigley's bloody face, then down to his bloody socks, and finally back to the cop. "He's here for tryouts," said the cop.

"Tryouts are just about over," Barnes said. "What's your name?" Barnes asked Wrigley.

"Wrigley Sanders."

Barnes smiled, turned away, rolled his eyes to the catcher, and then looked back down at his clipboard, and his eye caught Wrigley's name. "Fred," he said, "Warm this young man up."

Fred and Wrigley went running to the mound.

"What do you throw?" Fred asked uncomfortably, clearly trying to avoid the obvious question about the fact that Wrigley looked like a soldier back from war.

Wrigley looked at him like he had been asked to sum up his life story. "Well," said Wrigley, "an Overall drop ball, a

Koufax curve, a Ryan fastball, slider, knuckle, and a couple of others that I'm not sure have names."

Fred nodded, gave Wrigley a sideways glance, and put a ball in his glove. He noticed the ambi-glove and looked up at Wrigley. "Who *are* you?" he asked.

Wrigley smiled and started warming up both his arms by spinning them in circles, "We gonna throw or what?" he asked.

Fred nodded and ran behind the plate. Wrigley closed his eyes and saw Koufax. When he opened his eyes, he felt transformed. He wound up, reared back with his left arm cocked like a sling shot, kicked, released, and threw a perfect twelve o'clock to six o'clock curveball that spun so hard and broke so much, Fred missed it by a foot.

"What was *that?*" yelled Fred.

Barnes looked over as Fred went chasing after the ball. Fred came back, tapped his mitt a few times, threw the ball back to Wrigley, and said dubiously, "Do that again."

Wrigley reared back and threw another Sandy curveball. This one broke even a little more, but Fred was ready and caught it—*barely*.

"Coach?" Fred yelled. "Coach! You gotta see this!"

Barnes looked over to an excited college kid, waving and yelling like a tsunami was about to hit the campus.

"Be right back, boys," he said to his outfielders. He jogged over toward Fred, looking irritated. "What's so damn important?"

Fred nodded to Wrigley, who was standing on the mound with closed eyes.

"What's he doing?" Barnes asked.

"You'll see," Fred said.

Wrigley wound up and snapped off another classic Koufax curve. Barnes turned into a mouth-breathing statue. "Does he have a heater?"

"Says he does," Fred said.

"Let's have a fastball!" Fred yelled to Wrigley.

Wrigley nodded and switched his mitt back and forth a few times.

"Now what the hell is he doing?" Barnes asked.

Fred shrugged and said, "Picking a side."

Wrigley had closed his eyes and saw Nolan Ryan. He took a deep breath and opened his eyes. He took a long, languid windup from the right side, leading with his hips, and came right over the top with a blazing, moving fastball that popped Fred's glove. Fred yelped involuntarily.

Barnes looked at Fred, cleared his throat, and trying not to betray any signs of being impressed, walked out toward Wrigley, whose blood now mixed into his perspiration; his face looked almost pink. Barnes saw the blood coming out of his socks and just shook his head.

"So," Barnes said, "is this some sort of gimmick?"

Wrigley looked up at him, his coke bottle glasses making his appearance all the more comical. Or horrifying. "Excuse me?"

"Throwing left, throwing right and…uh…all this?" Barnes waved his arms up and down like a magician presenting his assistant.

Wrigley looked down at himself and back to Barnes, his naïve expression almost convincing Barnes that what seemed nothing short of a Jesus hopping off the cross to throw a couple of pitches that could've put him on Major League roster might not after all be an act.

"Had a little car accident on the way here," Wrigley slowly said.

"Okay. Tell you what," Barnes said, shaking his head back and forth. "Why don't you get cleaned up and come back and toss a few to some of our players tomorrow?"

"Yes, sir," Wrigley said excitedly, his crooked-toothed smile and tilted glasses glaring in the sunlight. He could make out a figure off in the distance, standing in a finely tailored suit. Even from here, Wrigley could definitely make out a big grin on Toothpick's face.

The next day, Biggs borrowed his mom's car and drove Wrigley back to the campus. Wrigley was wearing his Cubs hat, with his uniform clean and white—ready for action.

This time, Coach Barnes sat behind the plate. He discovered quickly that the kid had more pitches than he had fingers.

"All right, Senestraro," Coach said to his starting leadoff hitter, "let's see if you can hit this guy."

Wrigley wound up with his Orval Overall motion and threw a beautiful drop ball that looked like a strike but at the last second hit the back of the plate while Senestraro swung over the top of the pitch.

"One more," Senestraro said, looking back at his coach. "One more!" he yelled at Wrigley.

Wrigley threw another drop ball. Senestraro swung over it again.

"Ok, ok, I got this," said Senestraro, digging in.

Senestraro saw the windup and anticipated another drop ball. He was right and resolved to lay off of it. But as it came in, it was just too juicy. It was like one sequence repeated three times.

"Strike three, Senestraro," said Barnes, chuckling. Senestraro looked back at his coach, more defeated than angry and walked away from the plate shaking his head.

"Buckley!" called Barnes. "Take a few cuts!"

Buckley took a few warm up swings just outside the batter's box. Wrigley noticed he was a lefty with a short swing who was certainly a contact hitter. From the calm expression on his face, he detected a pretty great one. Barnes pumped his mitt a couple times and gave Wrigley his target. Wrigley looked in for the sign and got the ol' number one. Wrigley flipped his glove over to his right hand. It was time to morph into Koufax.

Buckley went down on three straight pitches: a 95-plus fastball on the inside of the plate, a twelve-to-six curve that had the hitter ducking out of the box, and finally, a low fastball on the outside corner. Before walking away from the plate, Buckley turned to his coach and flashed him a smile. "Unhittable," he said.

"Ya think?" returned Barnes, grinning behind the catcher's mask.

Sanderson thrust the knob of his bat into the dirt to release the warm-up donut from the barrel and strutted out to the plate. Sanderson had arms the size of most people's legs, and when he got to the batter's box, warmed up with a swing Wrigley interpreted as slightly overconfident.

Coach Barnes sat behind the plate with a grin on his face. He knew exactly what Sanderson was thinking. He also knew that Sanderson wouldn't be able to even foul off one of those drop balls, let alone hit it out of the park. Coach Barnes dropped down the sign for a drop ball, his hand pointing to the ground with his fingers together. Wrigley flipped his mitt over to his left hand, closed his eyes, saw Overall in his mind's eye, opened his eyes, and came to set.

The pitch looked to Sanderson like a big, slow volleyball coming over the plate. Sanderson swung with all his might and missed by a mile. "What the f— was that?" he asked his coach.

"A drop ball," said Coach Barnes. "And watch your mouth."

"Is it legal?"

"Yup."

"It shouldn't be," said Sanderson taking a couple of practice cuts.

Two more drop balls hypnotized Sanderson. Like Senestraro, the part of his brain that told him to lay off gave way to the part that saw a juicy rib eye.

"Make sure *we* get him coach," Sanderson said as he walked away from the plate, his eyes affixed to the ground. Coach Barnes got up and walked slowly to the mound. He'd been a pro catcher in his day, before his knee injury, and he'd never seen anyone throw like Wrigley.

"Son," Coach said, "where'd you learn to throw like that?"

Wrigley, grinning from ear to ear said, "My grandpa was a pitching coach for the Cubs and I…well…he taught me. I love pitching. My mom says I'm gonna be a closer for the Cubbies!"

Coach Barnes looked at him curiously, then smiled and stuck out his hand. "Well, you've got yourself a spot on *this* team," he said. "Congratulations."

★ ★ ★

Wrigley started kicking the dirt, trying to block out the air horn. He wished Annie would've left it at home. She sat in the stands, almost too nervous to press the air horn's button.

"You got this, Wrigs!" she screamed.

Toothpick, wearing a dapper suit with his signature piece of wood wiggling in his mouth, just couldn't stop grinning. The Lasaine Gang—each and every one of them was there—watched as Wrigley finally took the mound for the Pepperdine Waves in the bottom of the 9th.

"Go get 'em, retard!" yelled Elliott. Biggs shot him a look. Elliott returned a rascally smile and shrugged his shoulders. *What'd I say?*

It was time to see what their four-eyed, duck-walking pitching chameleon could do in a game-time situation, thought Coach Barnes. And quite a situation it was with Pepperdine ahead by one and archrival Fullerton's All-American leadoff man Meyhew, already three for three, coming up. Wrigley dug in and got the sign. A Koufax curve.

"Here we go, Papa," he whispered. He came to set, took a deep breath, and unleashed a twelve-to-six curve. The hitter bailed out.

"Strike one!" cried the umpire. Meyhew looked behind the plate, not sure if he should be angry about the call or ask the umpire for help. Toothpick almost swallowed his wood. Annie blew the horn until the contraption ran out of gas. Even Elliott clapped until his hands hurt—and that was only the first strike. Wrigley threw another. Same pitch, same break, same result.

"Strike two!"

Fred noticed goose bumps on Meyhew's forearms. "He's gonna throw another," Fred told the hitter.

"What?" asked Meyhew, looking back at Fred, a tremor in his voice.

"The Koufax curve," he said. "He's gonna throw another."

"Yeah, sure," said Meyhew, digging in.

"Just trying to give you a fair chance," said Fred as he dropped two fingers. Wrigley grinned like a Cheshire cat, nodded, and came to set. Meyhew saw from the windup and position of Wrigley's arm that Fred was telling the truth. He resolved to hang in, be patient, as the pitch looked like it was going to circumvent, the curve was so pronounced.

Wait…wait…wait…

"Strike three!" called the umpire. Meyhew just stood there, petrified, like a statue. Fred stood up and chucked the ball down to the third baseman so it could make its way around the horn. "I tried to…"

"Save it," interrupted Meyhew through gritted teeth as he stalked back to the dugout.

Annie stamped her feet, and frustratingly pushed down hard on the button of her dead air horn. The whole crowd was going nuts.

"Who *is* that guy?" the man next to Annie said to no one in particular.

"My son!" she nearly screamed.

Fred came out to the mound and asked Wrigley which pitch he wanted to start out the next batter.

"Knuckler," he said, switching his glove to his left hand. It was the only pitch that he did not model after another pitcher. He didn't dig his nails into the ball, or even press his fingers on the ball. He actually pushed it toward the plate, like he was hitting a bully with a level karate punch. The ball left all parts of his hand at the same time with the end result an unconventional pitch that did not spin an inch and wiggled a lot, and moved so much that his Lasaine Gang catcher, Work; his high school catcher, Martin; Coach Barnes; and even Toothpick—who could, like a magician, handle nearly all of Wrigley's pitches *with ease*—had a hard time catching it. But Fred, he almost always held on.

The ball came out of Wrigley's hand and sailed through the air in slow motion without a whiff of a spin. It jumped left, then right, shot up, then down, and finally landed right in the middle of Fred's mitt with a soft thud.

"Strike!" the umpire yelled.

The batter came out of the box and looked long and hard at Wrigley. Wrigley didn't see him. He was standing on the mound with his eyes closed—flashing through Wilhelm, Niekro, and Perry, all of whom were in the blender that became this googly-eyed milkshake.

He opened his eyes, got his grip, and started his windup, which, with its subtle motion—especially compared to his elaborate Koufax kick—told the batter *exactly* what was coming.

"Two!" yelled the umpire. The hitter stepped out again, then stepped back in and moved forward in the batter's box. Wrigley noticed the change in footwork; so did Fred.

The hitter was shortening up, preparing to drive the ball through the infield. It was time for the Ryan Express. Wrigley stood a little taller, stronger, and by the time the hitter noticed the power windup, threw a fierce, over-the-top four-seam spin fastball that made cement blocks of his legs.

"Three, *yaw!*" barked the umpire.

Fred leaped up in the air and hustled out to the mound where he placed the ball firmly in Wrigley's glove and placed his glove hand around the back of Wrigley's head. "Yeah, kid, yeah!"

The rest of the team hustled out to the mound with each member waiting to shake the hand of their new oracle. Wrigley was the happiest he'd ever been as one player after another grabbed his hand, arm, or shoulder and shook it vigorously. In the celebratory commotion, one of the players grabbed Wrigley's left hand—pulled and twisted his arm with a sharp jolt. Wrigley instinctively pulled his arm away, the smile disappearing. He shook it out, rotated it a couple times, and felt nothing. He shook his head slightly, breathed a sigh of relief, and continued to let himself be engulfed.

The next morning, Wrigley's left elbow looked like it had a softball growing out of it.

"Mom! MOM!" he yelled from the bathroom.

Annie ran into the bathroom. "What the hell?" she said. Wrigley had a horrified look on his face as he lifted his left arm with the support of his right and displayed it for his mom.

She scrutinized it, and even though she saw this wasn't good, forced a slight smile. "I'm sure it's nothing," she said. "Just a bruise or something. I'll get you some ice."

When she got to the kitchen, she dialed Toothpick's number and explained what she saw.

"I'm on my way," Toothpick moaned.

"Six pitches…" Toothpick said to himself as he examined Wrigley's arm.

"I felt something funny when one of my teammates grabbed my left hand after the game," Wrigley said. "He twisted it, just for a second, then it…"

"*Twisting*," Toothpick interrupted looking up at the ceiling. His eyes darted back and forth between Wrigley's eyes and his arm. "We're going to see Dr. Heron today," he said, then looking up at Annie, "Twisting is never good."

CHAPTER 16

"Folks," Vinny said. "What you just saw was a spot-on imitation of good old Johnny Kucks. Kucks was a big Yankee pitcher, six foot three, and it's said his strength came from eating meat his dad brought home from his job at the Hoboken meat packing company."

Wrigley got the ball back from the catcher and looked back at Kucks. Kucks did his whole windup in slow motion, at one point exaggerating the snap of his wrist, showing how to end his delivery. Wrigley waved a thank you to Kucks and threw another pitch. This time he snapped off a stinking nasty sinkerball right over the inside corner. At the last moment, it dropped a good four inches. But Lou Gehrig, making the necessary adjustments, somehow made contact and smacked a groundball hard up the middle, just right of second base, heading for the outfield. A blur came from the second base side. Evers grabbed the ball with his bare hand and quickly tossed it over second base. Tinkers snapped it up, and the inning was over.

As Wrigley left the field, he saw the ghostly image of a Greek man with a goat happily standing and watching the game. It had to be William "Billy Goat" Cianis, Wrigley thought. Cianis actually smiled and waved at Wrigley. Wrigley smiled and waved back.

★ ★ ★

Black Patty, with his bright white skin, giant red 'fro, and freckled face was the first to visit. Wrigley's arm was wrapped up like a miniature mummy. "How you doin', man?" he asked.

"They said I may not be able to throw with the left again," said Wrigley, his eyes starting to water.

"Nah," dismissed Black Patty, giving him a friendly knock on the cast. Wrigley winced. "Sorry, Wrigs!" he said stroking the cast. "Sorry."

"I could try going just righty," said Wrigley, "but I just don't know what I'll do if I have to send Koufax into an early retirement—*again*."

Patty gave Wrigley a quizzical look.

"You know," said Wrigley, "Koufax. Arm trouble. Done by 30."

"Bummer," Patty said, shrugging. "Hey," he said, "mind if I…?"

"Help yourself," Wrigley interrupted, rolling his eyes. "You know where they are."

Patty smiled and walked into the kitchen, opened up the fridge, and pulled out a half a gallon of milk. Then he went to the shelf that held the Oreo cookies. It was a ritual that Patty did most every time he entered the Sanders's home. But this time, he had the decency to pour a couple of glasses and put the cookies on a plate.

"Listen, Wrigs," Patty said, putting Wrigley's glass on a table right by his right arm and offering him the plate, "do you want to come work for us in the boiler room?"

Black Patty worked in a phone room selling candy all across the country. He always joked about how many crazy characters worked for his dad and how much money they made.

"Dad said you could come on whenever you want, for as long as you like," Black Patty softly said. "Figured with your arm out of commission for a while, you may need to fill the time. It's just four-hour shifts, and you'll make some cold cash."

"I ah…I don't know…" Wrigley said, looking down at his arm. "I need to rehab."

"Aw, c'mon…" Black Patty said, "You'd fit right in. Come on down, spend four hours, meet some of the crew. It's actually fun. It won't keep you from being a pitcher."

Wrigley thought long and hard. *It won't keep you from being a pitcher.* Black Patty was the ultimate salesman. He knew *exactly* what Wrigley was thinking. But what if he took this job, met a woman, had two kids before he even pitched another game. *Not for me*, thought Wrigley. *Papa gave up on his dream and spent the rest of his life regretting it, wondering how it would have been if he hadn't given up on his dream of coaching in pro baseball.* Just then, Annie came around the corner and saw Wrigley standing in a daze, contemplating something. Then she turned and looked at the half-eaten bag of Oreos, at Black Patty who was smiling broadly, displaying a mouth full of Oreo teeth. She shot him a smile and shook her head then continued on into the kitchen.

"Hey, Wrigs," Black Patty said, shaking Wrigley out of his daydream. "I think she likes me!"

"Oh yeah?" said Wrigley, unsuccessfully stifling a smile.

"So you wanna come meet the gang?" Black Patty asked. "You'll make some extra cash to help pay for your rehab."

Wrigley bit his lip, took a breath, then nodded "yes," thinking, *What the heck, I'm going to be on the DL for at least half a year. Maybe this will make the time go by faster.*

The next week Black Patty brought Wrigley to work. In a long, narrow room with low-hanging ceilings and poor lighting sat about 50 out-of-work actors, punk rockers, tattooed bikers–all of them huddled in their own small cubicles, on the phone, hawking candy.

"Come on now, Floyd. I onlee askin' ya fo' two barrels o' black and two o' red," the twenty-something punk rocker with jet-black spiked hair, huge silver hoop earrings, and eye-brows bleached white drawled Southern style as slow as molasses. "I knows you don't like the red, but yo' customahs do. Cum ooon…" he slowly urged. "You know daay gonna love 'em… Dat a boy, Floyd. Now yoo steppin' up!"

The rocker gave Patty the thumbs-up sign, covered the phone and said in a rapid-fire, crisp, unaccented voice, "Got 'em for two barrels instead of one. Bonus time, baby!"

"Keep up the good work, Ted," Black Patty said with a smile and kept walking down the aisle with Wrigley. Wrigley looked at Patty questioningly.

"Ted's working the South," he said. "So he slows down his talk, takes on the accent of his customer, and lands a lot more sales that way. I've heard him with a very strong Brooklyn accent, Canadian—I heard him talking to a guy from Boston, and Ted's accent was thicker than his customer's."

Wrigley raised his eyebrows and nodded his head, impressed.

"We listen in on the conversations," Patty said. "That's about all I do these days—monitor calls to make sure the gang here is doing their job and isn't breaking any laws."

"That guy was *great*," Wrigley said. "I can't do that."

"You don't have to. Ted's one of our best. It comes to you over time. He's been here 10 years. He's also the leader of a band called *Adulterous Boys*. Wrigley looked at him dubiously. "Never mind," said Patty.

They came to the end of a long hallway, and there sat Wrigley's cubicle: it had a single phone, a pad of paper, and a messy pile of leads on bright yellow paper.

"You'll start with the reject leads," Black Patty said. "These are the old or rarely sold leads that are extremely hard to close. You'll get turned down a lot; no one expects anything so there's no pressure. Just have fun. It's practice. Like spring training. A win-win." Black Patty looked at his watch. "Lunchtime! What do you say I treat you to a Cavaretta's meatball sandwich?"

The deli was just around the corner from the boiler room in Canoga Park.

"What's up?" Black Patty yelled out to Gianni behind the counter.

"The usual, Patty?" Gianni yelled back, not breaking his sandwich-making stride. "Hey, Wrigs!" he said, nodding at Wrigley. Black Patty looked at Wrigley like he had trespassed on his haunt.

"What?" Wrigley shrugged. "Mom and I like the cannoli. We come here a lot."

"Good taste. You know, Wrigs," said Patty, as they waited for their sandwiches, "ninety-nine out of a hundred new hires don't last more than a month." Wrigley looked interested.

"One word says it all, Wrigs," said Patty, "Rejection. They're spooked by the word 'no.'"

"Two meatball sandwiches," Gianni said, slamming them on the table between Wrigley and Patty. "What's ya drinkin' today, Patty?"

"Root beer," Patty said.

"And you, Wrigs?"

"Make it two," Wrigley said flashing a peace sign. They both took big bites into the hot and saucy sandwich.

"Anyway," said Patty, his mouth full. "That's the truth of the matter. One in a hundred, Wrigley."

As the two friends shoveled their sandwiches down their throats, two Italian cannoli pastries—their ends covered in chocolate sprinkles—appeared on their table.

"Thanks, Gianni," Wrigley said, through a mouthful of sandwich.

"You'll do just fine," Patty laughed. "Juuuuust fiiiiine…"

★ ★ ★

"We recommend two barrels of red and two of black," said Wrigley.

"Well," said the national sales manager of the Coors Corporation, "we have a number of displays all across the country, son. But we sell beer not licorice."

The fact that after 50 calls, he had someone willing to talk with him was enough for Wrigley to get creative. "What if…" he said, biting his lip and rolling his eyes up to his right brain, "…what if you have a couple of barrels of licorice sitting on your display with a sign that says 'Free'? I don't much discriminate when it comes to beer, but if you offer me free candy, you can bet I'll start discriminatin'" Wrigley wasn't sure where that came from—*you can bet I'll start discriminatin'*—but he waited out the long silence.

"You know, son," the Coors manager said, "that makes sense. We have about two thousand displays, so I'm thinking we'll get four sets of red and black for each display—eight thousand sets…"

"Wait, what?" Wrigley said, "Are you sure?"

"Is my math wrong?" asked the manager earnestly.

Wrigley realized he was serious. "Yes, I mean no. Thank you, sir. Thank you very, very much!" Wrigley wrote up all the paperwork, closed the deal, and took a deep breath.

"How's it goin' Wrigs?" asked Black Patty, coming by to check on him about ten minutes after he got off the phone. Wrigley, still a little in shock, was just staring at the order form.

Patty looked down at the order and his eyes got big—really big. "What the…? *How* the…? Eight thousand sets?"

Black Patty picked up the order form and the yellow lead sheet and raced off.

"I'll be back," he yelled over his shoulder. "Gotta talk to Dad." Patty returned in about ten minutes with a smile on his face. "You're going to be the top producer this month!" he said, out of breath. "On your first day…"

Wrigley looked confused. "Wait, you mean, from one call?"

"Yes, Wrigs! I told you! I knew it!"

Black Patty excitedly took off down the aisle like he had made the sale himself. He bumped right into a leather-clad, bleached blond punk-rock woman who had five sets of earrings in each ear, a nose ring, and bright red lipstick.

"Watch it, freckles. What you so happy about, boss man?" she said.

"My guy," he said, dramatically pointing a thumb at himself then toward Wrigley, "just landed his first account and it was a big'un!" Patty continued his victory lap toward his father's office. The mod woman looked over at Wrigley's cubicle and strutted on over there.

"First account, huh?" she said, interrupting Wrigley's reverie.

"Yeah," he said, startled. "Eight thousand sets—to Coors."

"You're lying, four eyes," she said.

"No, no," Wrigley said, "Look…"

She looked at the carbon copy of the order. It appeared to be real. "What's your name, gorgeous?" she asked.

"Wrigley," he responded sticking out his hand. "Wrigley Sanders. And you are…?"

"How'd you get that name?" she responded, offering up her own hand but ignoring the question.

"It's a long story," Wrigley said. "Tell you about it over a…a…cannoli?"

"Cindy," she said, answering the previous question and dubiously nodding her head to the current one. "Cindy Zakarek. Sure, I'd love a cannoli."

At Cavaretta's, Wrigley ordered the cannoli and excused himself to go to the bathroom. He looked in the mirror and nervously scrutinized his face for leftover lunch on the corners of his lips and pimples on his sweaty forehead. He then gripped the sides of the sink, looking straight down at the drain, took a deep breath, looked up again at himself, smiled, and nodded. On his way out of the restroom, he came upon a picture of Phil Cavaretta, the deli's namesake, on the wall—a big, poster-sized picture of the pro baseball player.

Phil Cavaretta, the plaque read. In 1935, at the young age of eighteen, our restaurant's founder became the Chicago Cubs' starting first baseman. He was voted the 1945 National League Most Valuable Player after leading the Cubs to the pennant while winning the batting title with a .355 average. His 20 seasons (1934–1953) played for the Cubs is the second-most in franchise history, behind Cap Anson. He managed the Cubs in his final three seasons with the club.

"You okay?" Cindy asked, coming around the corner, startling Wrigley. "Thought maybe you had fallen in…What's with the guy?"

"Phil Cavaretta," he said. "Was a Cub great."

"Wow," Cindy said, a little sarcastically. "Twenty years. That's a long time to work for one company. Can we eat our cannoli now? I'm starved."

"Okay," Wrigley said, laughing.

While they ate, he told her about his playing career; how he hurt his arm; how once he got better, he was going to be a closer for the Cubs.

"Sounds to me like you're already a closer on the phone," Cindy said. "Eight thousand bucks. That must be a record commission."

Wrigley blushed. She didn't care much about baseball, but the fact that the cannoli tasted extra good today must account for the company. This goofy kid with the duck walk was cute.

"Wanna catch a drink at Vern's tonight?" Cindy asked Wrigley, interested in a second date.

"Yeah!" Wrigley said, a little too excited. "I mean, if you're free."

Cindy smiled and shook her head and thought, *Yeah, the kid was cute.*

★ ★ ★

Vern's pub was a hole in the wall known for its burgers, cheap tap beer, and darts. After a few beers and small talk, Cindy wanted to know more about Wrigley's past.

"So you washed out of college, eh?" Cindy asked.

"Well, kinda. I blew out my arm. I was on a baseball scholarship, so we're not sure what's next. I don't even know if

I've got what it takes to pitch in the majors. But all that doesn't really matter if my arm doesn't heal. Time will tell. In the meantime, Patty was kind enough to offer me a job. How long have you been selling candy?"

"Six years," Cindy said, affecting an exhausted face. Clearly she was burned out. "I dropped out of high school. Ran away with my boyfriend to Hawaii. Then…well, let's just say it didn't work out. And here I am."

"I've never had a girlfriend," Wrigley said, then quickly regretted it. "Sorry," he said planting a palm on his forehead. "Don't know why I said that."

"That's okay," Cindy said quickly, putting a hand on his. "I find that refreshing."

"Is your hair real?" Wrigley asked, then made an embarrassed face like he had put the other foot in his mouth. But Cindy couldn't contain her laughter, leaning back and nearly falling off her stool. She then leaned forward, grabbed Wrigley's right hand, and brought it through her hair.

It was real, real soft, thought Wrigley. "How do you keep it so white?" he asked.

"Dye it once a week," she said. She leaned up toward Wrigley's face and gave him a kiss on the lips.

"Wow," Cindy said. "I can hear your heart beating, four eyes. "

"Can we do that again?"

Cindy nodded and leaned in once more.

CHAPTER 17

"Folks," Vin Scully drawled, "Again, I have never seen the likes of Wrigley Sanders. He just struck out the side. His team is leaving the field, and he's still on the mound, waving to someone in the stands. Here comes the umpire again."

Wrigley gave one last wave to Billy Cianis and turned to watch a black cat cross the field, in the exact spot where one had crossed while the Cubbies were playing the Amazing Mets. *That cat*, thought Wrigley, *had cursed the Cubbies and made them lose their chance at the playoffs after being in first place most of the season.*

"Wrigley, you okay? That's three outs," said the umpire, giving Wrigley a little nudge and ushering Wrigley off the field. But on his way out, Wrigley saw another ghost of seasons past—Steve Bartman was leaning over the left field railing, ready to reach out for a fly ball.

"What the hell is going on?" Wrigley said out loud. The umpire looked at him with a smile and said, "Your team is up to bat. You pitched a clean inning in the World Series. Welcome to the big leagues."

★ ★ ★

"I'd like to thank all of you for your efforts over the last decade," Wrigley said standing in front of his crew he supervised at Cavaretta's. "Black Patty, guess you were right. Once you make that first sale, everything else just falls into place."

"It *was* a rather large sale," Black Patty joked, with the whole crowd laughing. "A lucky one at that—for all of us."

Wrigley's giant Coors commission was now part of the company's legend and a part of his monthly commission check that was quite hefty. The Coors sales manager had reported back that his beer sales had tripled, so he continued to order more and more sets of licorice for his ever-increasing end tables of beer. The money became huge, and before Wrigley knew it, *ten years* had flown by in a blink!

Now, new hires were told all about Wrigley's first day on the job, and typical of the management's generous fashion, they started making sure that commercial leads were in the newcomer pile. "You, too, could hit a home run" became the company's theme.

After the presentation, Wrigley and Cindy took the whole crew to Vern's Pub to celebrate their upcoming bonus for out-producing the past generation of sales teams. Wrigley's team was a full 20 percent higher than any other team had been at this point in time.

"I bet you can't throw five bulls eyes in a row," Cindy challenged Wrigley.

"How much?" yelled Wrigley, a little too loud, after having drunk a few beers.

"Another beer," she said.

"And five kisses," he said. Cindy smiled and nodded.

"Pay up," he said, smiling, after hitting five for five, the last with his eyes closed.

Cindy, now sporting jet-black hair and still looking punk in the extreme, even though she was a mom, very dramatically strutted over to Wrigley and puckered her bright red lipstick-covered lips. She proceeded to give Wrigley five huge smooches, freshening up her lipstick in between each. The crew was laughing hysterically. Wrigley's face, neck, and bald forehead were covered with bright, shiny, perfectly formed, red, lip marks.

"Double or nothing?" Cindy said, after pulling away from Wrigley's neck.

"What?" Wrigley laughed. "You already paid up."

"Okay. So. I double the bet." Cindy giggled. "You hit 5 more bulls eyes—lefty—and you get ten."

"Can I wind up?" Wrigley asked.

"I wouldn't have it any other way," said Cindy. "Show us some of that Koufax magic. But if you lose," Cindy laughed, "I get a full body massage." Wrigley blushed. It had been over ten years since Wrigley had even considered throwing left handed. Cindy handed him the first of his darts and nodded toward the dartboard. His left hand was clammy as he took the dart.

Wrigley stepped to the thrower's line. A crowd of about 20 employees watched as Wrigley waddled off the rubber then came back to his thrower's line, treating it like a pitcher's mound.

When his foot hit the rubber, Wrigley changed posture, changed movement. He wound up, in dramatic Koufax fashion, stretching his arm way back with his right leg raised high and flying toward the plate. The dart came out of his arm in a flash and landed with a loud bang right in the bull's eye.

"Holy shit!" someone yelled. The rest remained silent, enthralled. Cindy smiled knowingly and handed Wrigley his next dart. Wrigley grinned his crooked-toothed grin, his glasses off center, his black bushy hair unruly, then approached the mound for a second time. Again, the same loud pop right in the center of the bull's eye. Three more identical outcomes, and a crowd of maybe 40 gathered around to witness what seemed otherworldly.

"You know who you remind me of?" said an older gentleman. "Sandy Koufax. Ever heard of him?"

Wrigley smiled and looked back at Cindy, whose face featured the very proud smile. "Honey. I think maybe you still owe me that full-body massage?" Cindy said. Wrigley nodded "yes."

★ ★ ★

The next morning, a Saturday, Wrigley got up, looked at the clock, let it tick just a few more minutes, then called Biggs. It was 6:04 a.m.

"Huh-llo?" Biggs groaned. Who that…?"

"Can you come over?" Wrigley said, cutting off Biggs.

"Wrigley?" he asked clearing his throat.

"Now? And bring your mitt."

"Wha…I…do you know what time…?" Biggs stumbled. "Sure."

Biggs sat at the side of his bed, rubbed his eyes, grabbed his Levi's and t-shirt off the side chair, and did a smell test. *C+*, he thought to himself. *Good enough.* He went to the bathroom, looked in the mirror, and tied back his slightly gray-streaked ponytail—a remnant of his band-touring days. He shook his head, not terribly satisfied with the condition of the face looking back at him. Hard rock 'n' roll living had gotten the best of him. He went into his closet and looked up at the highest shelf. He jumped up and grabbed the corner of a towel. Down came his glove, passing right through his hands and hitting him square on the face. He chuckled at the irony. When he arrived at Wrigley's, he found his aging friend pacing back and forth in the backyard, dressed in full 1908 Cubs regalia.

"Boy," he said, "it's been a long time since I've seen that uni. Looks a little tight, buddy."

Wrigley smiled and waved Biggs over to the plate. Ten years of thoughts ran through Biggs' head, one of them that Wrigley really was gonna throw again after all this time—but in a semi-sleep-walking state. Biggs shrugged his shoulders and complied. They warmed up playing catch for a good five minutes without a word as the sun began to light up the backyard. As he felt the sun warming his face, Biggs started to feel something like elation. Wrigley motioned for Biggs to get down into a squat. Then, after a little self-talk, Wrigley's eyes rolled back into focus and he threw a bullet that popped Biggs' glove.

"*Yow!*" shouted Biggs, now completely alert. "The Koufax. But your arm…I thought…"

"It's back," Wrigley said, smiling, "*I'm* back. And I'm gonna be a closer for the Cubs."

CHAPTER 18

Wrigley, still a little dazed, stumbled off the field and landed on the cold, hard bench.

"Folks," Vinny said. "That was simply amazing. I've never seen a pitcher come out of nowhere, pitch on center stage in the World Series, and close out an inning against three of the best Yankee hitters. Off we go, to the bottom of the 13th. The Cubbies are down one run, and right about now, millions of Cubs fans have to be asking the question: can their lovable losers win this game and end the suffering?

Wrigley was up next, and they couldn't hit for him, since nobody was left on the bench. The camera panned to Wrigley, who was in the on-deck circle taking Babe Ruth-worthy rips.

★ ★ ★

"Dad, you comin?" called out Wrigley's eight-year-old son, Ernie Banks Sanders.

"Did I ever tell you the one about King Kelly?" Wrigley said poking his head around the doorframe, his two boys who were in bunk beds, ready for a good bedtime story.

"No," said his six-year-old Fergie Jenkins Sanders from the top bunk.

"*Well*," Wrigley said dramatically, settling down next to the boy's bed. "King Kelly was not unlike my Grandpa Kelly. He was—*spirited*."

The boys—Ernie sitting cross-legged, Fergie on his belly resting his chin in his hands—fixed their eager eyes on Wrigley.

"The King could really hit," he said. "Back in 1880, he helped the Cubbies win five National League pennants. He led the league in 1884 hitting .354, and in 1886, he hit .388."

The boys' eyes became wide with disbelief.

"Oh yeah," said Wrigley "But the coolest thing he did was that he stole two bases at a time."

"How'd he do *that*?" asked Fergie.

"He's kidding," chimed in Ernie. "That's not possible…"

"Back in those days, they only had one umpire," said Wrigley. "So King, he'd be on first base, and if the ball was hit to deep right, the ump would run down the line to see if it was fair. King would take a peak over his shoulder, and if the ump wasn't looking, he'd cut the corner right behind the mound and go from first to third. He'd be pumping his arms, looking at the crowd, clowning around as they cheered him on. Sometimes, he'd even do this from second to home, running right past the pitcher, who would try and yell at the umpire, but they didn't hear because the crowd was noisy and they were way out in the outfield trying to see if the ball was fair or not."

"Wow," said Ernie.

"Yup" Wrigley smiled. "He was quite a character. And even though he stretched a single into a triple every now and again, he was inducted into the Hall of Fame in 1945. King Kelly—he was probably one of the best players of his day."

Wrigley looked up at the Cubs clock on the wall. "All right, boys," he said, standing from his chair. "Lights out."

"One more, Dad!" they both said in unison. "Please!"

Wrigley threw his hands up in mock frustration and said, "Okay, okay. How about Tinkers to Evers to Chance?"

"That's my favorite!" said Ernie.

"Mine, too" said Fergie.

"Here we go!" Wrigley said, "So the double play team of Tinkers to Evers to Chance started out when…

CHAPTER 19

"See you tonight, Mom," Wrigley said the next morning as he got up from the kitchen table.

"Ever hear the one about Dummy Hoy?" Annie asked weakly as Wrigley opened the screen door.

"Sorry?" he responded.

"Dummy Hoy," she repeated. "You ever hear of Dummy Hoy?"

"No, Mom, I haven't. Papa wanted to tell me that one. Can we talk tonight? I have to…"

"Been saving it for the right moment," Annie said as she stood up from the kitchen table, labored, and waved him in to the living room as she sat down on the couch.

"Mom," Wrigley said, "I really have to…"

"Back in 1903," Annie started, "William Ellsworth 'Dummy' Hoy—yeah, they called him 'Dummy'—played for the championship Angels. He hit .257 with 48 stolen bases and led the Pacific Coast League in runs."

"Not a great average," Wrigley said, sitting down next to Annie.

"Dummy made the best of what he had," Annie said. "They called him Dummy cause he couldn't hear or speak."

Wrigley raised his eyebrows.

"Got meningitis when he was three," she said. "Didn't use hearing aids. Dummy's why umpires use hand signals for balls and strikes. He invented the signs cause he couldn't hear them call out a pitch."

With this bit of information, Wrigley settled in to his chair, transforming back into a little boy right before Annie's eyes.

"He was a tough one," she went on. "He followed his dreams! Played all 212 games the Los Angeles Angels played in the PCL and had a lifetime average of .287. He hit the first ever grand slam in the American league. You're a lot like him, Wrigley, 'cept of course, you're gonna be a *closer* for the Cubbies. Why not, right?"

"Right now I have to be a closer at work," Wrigley joked.

"Follow your dreams, Wrigley. Papa didn't and he paid a big price," Annie said. Then she closed her eyes and laid her head back on a pillow.

"Okay, okay," Wrigley said half-heartedly, looking more at the door than his mom. "I promise, I'll try out for the Cubs when the time is right."

Wrigley got up, turned, and looked at Annie to say goodbye. She had a slight smile on her face but seemed more relaxed than Wrigley had ever seen her. He felt a shiver go down his spine, "Mom?"

★ ★ ★

"It's ridiculous," Wrigley said to Cindy as they were driving back from Annie's funeral. "I can't just try out for the Cubs. I'm not 20 years old anymore!"

"No, you're not," Cindy said with a smile. "Tell them you're 27."

"What! Who would? I can't think about it right now…" Wrigley said. "You sure the kids are going to be okay with Biggs?"

"They'll be fine. He promised to get them ice cream," Cindy said. "How about you?"

Wrigley didn't answer. He wanted to put on his Cubbie jammies like when he was a kid.

He'd sit down on his bed, rock back and forth and slam his head on the headboard; maybe that's why they call it that, he'd thought to himself. But no, he wasn't a kid anymore; he was a grown up, and he was going to deal with his mother's death with dignity.

"I know you're hurting, honey. But it's what she would've wanted," said Cindy, snapping Wrigley out of his daydream. "How many times did your mom say, 'My son's gonna be a closer for the Cubbies'?" In the last bit, Cindy did her best imitation of Annie.

Wrigley looked up at Cindy, first angry, then despairing. Tears came to his eyes. "That's exactly what she said."

Cindy shrugged, held her hands out and tossed Wrigley a big smile, "If you don't try," she said, putting a hand over Wrigley's, "you'll never forgive yourself. From the day I met you, that's all I've been hearing about. I don't understand it, but…"

He pulled up to a red light and looked over at Cindy, with her pierced nose, ears and jet-black hair. She was beautiful. He leaned in and kissed her gently on the cheek.

"Nice try. Don't change the subject," she said, jokingly pushing him away. "Call that coach guy."

★ ★ ★

"No," Toothpick said abruptly over FaceTime on his iPhone. "Wrigs, I'm truly sorry about your mom's passing, but the answer is still no!"

"Why not?" Wrigley asked.

"Because you're 33."

"I'll tell them I'm 27."

"Wrigley," Toothpick said with a sigh, "I love ya, but I know you're out of shape—and you haven't thrown in years."

"Not true. I've been throwing my regular routine lately," Wrigley said.

"Just to get a tryout?"

"Got one!" Wrigley interrupted.

"Excuse me?"

"They're having an open tryout," Wrigley said with extreme confidence. "I'm going to blow them all away and make the team!"

"There are gonna be tens, maybe *hundreds* of 95-mile-per-hour throwing 20-year-olds who are gonna be told to take a hike. Like I said, I love ya, but…"

"I quit my job," Wrigley said bashfully. "I've been working out hard."

"What?"

"I'm all in. I even got a Cubs tattoo—a big one…"

"Wrigley," Toothpick said, "are you out of your…?"

Wrigley took off his shirt just for a second, flashed his huge Cubs logo tattoo to Toothpick over the phone, then quickly put his shirt back on, a little embarrassed at how out of shape he was.

"…outta your mind?" Toothpick finished.

Wrigley's body was a mess. His belly hung over his belt. He legs were heavy and not particularly strong looking. His arms, well, they were fit looking. He did throw most of his life. But he looked like the last person you'd think would be hoping to go pro in Major League Baseball. *The last person*, thought Toothpick.

"I gotta go for it," Wrigley solemnly said. "I promised Mom."

"Good lord," Toothpick said with resignation. There was a long pause. "My father," chuckled Toothpick. "You kind of remind me of him. He was another Don Quixote. Okay, okay, meet me at Pepperdine. Tomorrow. Seven sharp. And Wrigley?"

"Yeah, Toothpick?"

"Bring your heat."

★ ★ ★

The next morning, Wrigley and Biggs pulled up to the Pepperdine Wave's practice field.

"How many years since you were here for the tryout," Biggs asked Wrigley.

"I can't count that high," Wrigley joked.

"Go ahead," Biggs said, motioning for Wrigley to head for the field, "I'll get my gear together and catch up."

Wrigley, in his 1908 Cubs gear, took a deep breath and opened the passenger side door. As he stepped out of the car, one of the buttons on his jersey popped off the bottom on his uniform near his belly. Wrigley watched it fly into the grass, paused for a moment, smiled, and decided to not even try and chase it down. Wrigley found Toothpick sitting in the stands reading a book. He had a radar gun next to him on the bench and a wood toothpick in his mouth.

"Hey, Wrigs," Toothpick said. "Do I get the pleasure of seeing it? I mean, getting a good long look at it?"

"I'll bring it," Wrigley said, looking at the radar gun. "Arm's ready."

"No," Toothpick said, tilting his head down and his eyes up toward Wrigley. "I mean the ink."

Wrigley blushed. "Riiiight," he said. "Well, I guess there's no surprises between us."

Wrigley peeled off his uniform, then his undershirt and revealed a bright, beautiful tattoo that started at the center of his chest and wrapped all the way around to the center of his back. It was a huge red, white, and blue Cubs logo with the word "Closer" right under his left breast. There was a big scar where his belly button had popped years ago and a truck-sized "spare tire" of fat around his waist.

"Closer," said Toothpick nodding, "Man, you went big." Toothpick moved closer and scrutinized Wrigley's torso. "And I must admit," he said, "it *is* some fine work."

"Thanks!" Wrigley said, excited to have won over his rather conservative mentor. "Cindy helped me to shave my back and chest and…"

"Okay. Enough! Let's warm it up," Toothpick said, dramatically pounding his catcher's mitt.

"I got this," said Biggs as he jogged up from the car.

Toothpick looked over, surprised. "Biggs? That you?"

"In the flesh," he said, offering Toothpick a royal bow.

After a brief warm-up, Biggs took Wrigley through his full repertoire of pitches, from Koufax to Marichal, from Charlie Root to Orval Overall, finishing off with a Nolan Ryan fastball that really popped the glove. When he was done, Wrigley noticed that Toothpick had dropped the radar gun and had a strange look on his face.

"Swallowed it," he muttered, pointing to his lips. Wrigley and Biggs looked confused.

"Whole toothpick."

"Naw," Wrigley said with a smile.

Toothpick nodded. "You hit 97 mph."

Wrigley just grinned. Biggs raised up a hand and gave him a high five.

"In the morning," Toothpick said. "We're going to see my friend Bud."

"Who's Bud?"

★ ★ ★

"You know, Wrigs," Toothpick said, on their way to San Diego the next morning, "fishing is a lot like pitching. When you fish, it's imperative each time you cast you truly believe there is a fish out there waiting for your fly. If you don't believe, even after hundreds of casts, you won't be ready when they finally bite. Each cast is the one."

Toothpick looked over at Wrigley, who looked confused. "The point is, each pitch has a purpose, Wrigs," he said clarifying, "and it's vital you believe it's going to hit its target and do its job. 'Cause in the Bigs, man, one mistake is all it takes."

"Kinda like the way Maddux pitched," Wrigley said, getting it.

"*Exactly!*" Toothpick said.

"So, can you tell me more about Bud?" Wrigley asked.

"You'll see," Toothpick said.

They pulled up to the warehouse. Inside was a huge room with four mounds and numerous cameras pointed at each one. A couple of pitchers were going through their routines and being filmed. Bud Clarkston, a heavy-set, balding man with a red bulb of a nose saw Toothpick. "Hey brother!" he called out to him, "Over here!"

"Hey Budda!" Toothpick called back. He then turned to Wrigley, who was laughing, smiling, and wondering who this "Budda" guy was. Toothpick surreptitiously signaled for Wrigley to follow him.

"So," said Bud smiling, as Toothpick and Wrigley came near, "this is the man."

"Yep," said Toothpick, looking at Wrigley proudly.

Bud noticed Wrigley's ambi-glove, scrutinized it, and looked up at Toothpick with surprise.

"When you said…I didn't think…I mean…I know you don't bullshit, but…"

"You want him to throw lefty or righty first?" said Toothpick, relieving Bud of ditch-digging duty.

"Um…lefty?" said Bud, shrugging his shoulders.

Toothpick took a ball from Bud's stupefied hand.

"Give him Koufax," Toothpick said, tossing the ball to Wrigley. He then pulled a catcher's mitt with an orange painted border from the waistband of his pants and tossed it to Bud. "Use this."

Wrigley moved to the rubber on an artificial mound. He dug in, and out of habit, looked for a sign. Bud returned a confused shoulder shrug. He went into his Koufax windup. Attuned to every little movement of his arms, legs, and back, he came toward the plate and felt the rotation of his hips, the whip-like catapult of his arm, and the follow through that ended with his left arm way over his right leg.

"Whoa!" Bud said, looking at Toothpick with raised eyebrows. "That went twelve to six."

"Like Koufax," Toothpick said with a smile.

"Like Koufax," Bud said in agreement.

Wrigley threw another twenty pitching including a Ryan Express, an Overall drop ball, and a Marichal heater—where he concealed the ball until the very last second and unleashed a bullet that knocked Bud onto his rear—and Bud had seen enough.

"He's the most athletic pitcher I've seen since Bartolo Colon. His body control, his delivery…I saw him morph into four completely different pitchers. Wait here!"

Bud disappeared into his office and returned with a five-page report. "He's a natural," Bud said, passing the pages to Toothpick. "He passed all my critical tests with flying colors. What a repertoire. And he has it all. Spin rate in top 5 percent. Velocity top 20 percent. First pitch strikes are off the charts! Everything!"

"You have what it takes, Wrigs," Toothpick said on the ride home. "When I first met you, I thought you had talent but I underestimated your drive. But you still need one more thing…"

"What's that?" Wrigley asked.

"A theme song," Toothpick said, turning to Wrigley, smiling.

That night, in his bathroom, after a long drive back from San Diego in bumper-to-bumper traffic, Wrigley looked in the mirror, at his big white belly covered with his bright Cubs tattoo and started belting out Tom Petty's *Won't Back Down*, butchering the words and the tune: "You can stand me up, but I won't back down. There's no way out…hey baby…won't back down."

"Honey," Cindy called out from bed. "Who sings that song?"

"Tom Petty," Wrigley said.

"Can we *please* keep it that way? Come to bed."

Wrigley took one last look in the mirror, examining his old-man body and smiled a ragged, toothy grin. "Coming!" he called back.

★ ★ ★

The following morning, Toothpick gave a call to an old friend of his, Les Harris, who worked in the Cubs bullpen. When Toothpick told him about Wrigley, he asked the usual questions about experience, control, and velocity. When Toothpick got to the age part, the coach's attitude dramatically changed.

"Sorry, Toothpick, I'm not interested in a guy "around" 30. With all these young guns…"

"I understand, Les," Toothpick said and thought, *maybe I should have said 27*. Then, "I promised this young lad's grandfather, Connor Kelly, I would do my best to get him a try out."

"Really? *Kelly's* Grandson."

"Yes," said Toothpick. "Know him?"

"Yes! Why didn't you say that in the first place? I wouldn't be here today without Connor's help. We go way back. I'll do it. But let's keep expectations real low. Okay? I mean, 30?"

"Thanks, Les," Toothpick said. "Oh, and did I mention he pitches with both arms?"

"Excuse me?" Les said.

★ ★ ★

A week later, Wrigley and Toothpick were in Mesa Arizona with Les for a personal tryout. Wrigley was asked to pitch to the Cubs' top prospect Eloy Jiminez. Wrigley, after putting on his old-time Cubs uniform in the locker room, got out his iPhone and hit play. *"You can stand me up, but I won't back down. There's no way out...hey baby...won't back down."*

Toothpick peaked around the door. "Hey," he said smiling. "Ready?"

Wrigley patted his mitt with his right hand and his left a few times and nodded toward the field. "We're about to find out," he said. With that, he carefully placed his hat atop his head and jogged toward the locker room exit, giving Toothpick a playful knock on the shoulder with his glove as he passed him.

"Here you go, Wrigs. Here you go," Toothpick muttered to himself.

On the field, the top prospect was warming up and hitting off the batting practice pitcher. Wrigley was in awe of the kid's swing. He couldn't find a weak spot.

"Over here," Les said from his place next to the batting cages. As Wrigley approached, Les noticed he looked older than Toothpick had sold him on, and out of shape. Nevertheless, Les reached out for Wrigley's hand. He noticed the long fingers and strong grip, and thought, *That's a grip that belongs to someone else, not this visually impaired Coke-bottle bespectacled kid.*

"I knew your granddad real well," Les said. "He was a fine baseball man."

"Thank you, sir," Wrigley said, flashing his crooked grin, looking through his goofy glasses, and rapidly brushing his black curly hair back underneath his hat.

"What's with the uniform?" Les said.

"What do you mean?" Wrigley asked, smiling. "I've been a Cubbie all my life."

"Get out there, kid," Les said, smiling back. "Rod!" he said, yelling out to the pitcher on the mound, "we're relieving you."

Les watched Wrigley from the back as his feet, sticking out like a duck's, waddled him toward the hill. He noticed Wrigley's substantial belly and back fat bounce along the way.

"How old did you say this dude was?" Les asked Toothpick as he approached the batting cage.

"Thirty-ish" Toothpick said, looking at Les out of the corner of his eye and grinning slightly. "Just let him throw." Les chuckled and adjusted his cap.

The prospect came up to the plate and took a couple of practice swings. Wrigley dug in, paused, and looked at Toothpick. *Koufax*, he mouthed. Victor Caratini, the bullpen catcher, put down a signal.

Wrigley smiled and closed his eyes. When he opened them, the prospect could only see the whites of his eyes. He wound up long and lean and threw…twelve straight strikes, mostly curves with a couple of 95-miles-an-hour fastballs mixed in. Not a ball was touched. Not even a foul. Twelve straight whiffs.

"Ryan!" Toothpick called out. Wrigley nodded and changed his composure, his stance, standing taller, changing his glove from his right hand to his left. He rocked back, raised his hands above his head, brought his knee to his chin while bringing his hands down to his abdomen, and launched a fastball that not only caused the prospect to swing late, it knocked him right off his feet.

"Holy mackerel!" Les said, looking into the bleachers to make sure no spies—scouts—were around. "I swear I just saw Donald Duck transform into the Express. Who *is* this kid?"

"Watch this," Toothpick whispered to Les. "Overall!" Toothpick called out to Wrigley.

Wrigley threw five straight Orval Overall drop balls coming in at about 75 miles per hour. Each one spun in near slow motion, and every time, the hitter swung a few inches above the ball. As the strikes piled up, the hitter tried harder and harder to make contact, changing his stance, his swing, dropping a knee to the ground, all to no avail.

"Okay," Les said to Toothpick. "Okay!" Les called out to Wrigley. Then to the dejected prospect, "Shake it off, Eloy, you'll learn from this." Then to no one in particular, "I think we all will."

Wrigley pretended not to see Les waving him in and continued digging at the rubber. He didn't want to leave. He liked how the mound was so manicured, just like the one in his—*Papa's*—backyard. Perfect. Toothpick walked out to retrieve him.

"What do you think?" Les said to Victor, the bullpen catcher, when Toothpick was at a safe distance.

"What are you nuts?" answered Victor. Then realizing the tone he was taking with his coach, "I mean, it's nuts. *He's* nuts."

"Yeah," said Les looking out at Wrigley. "Nuts." He grabbed Victor by the catcher's mask. "But he's *our* nut." Les put his face right up against Victor's mask and looked into his eyes. "You didn't see this today, got it? You don't say a single word about this to anyone—your wife, your dog, nobody. This DID NOT HAPPEN."

"Y…y…yeah, Coach," stuttered Victor.

"Hey, Wrigley!" Les called to Wrigley who still stood on the mound, fixing the dirt between the rubber and home plate. Wrigley looked up to find Les springing toward him. "Not bad, kid, not bad."

"Not bad," said Toothpick exaggeratedly. "I think the question is, are you gonna sign him or are we gonna have to go to St. Lou…"

"Let's get this boy a physical A.S.A.P.! I'll talk to Theo, and rest assured, we will lock this down."

★ ★ ★

"He has the arms of a 25-year-old and the body of a 40-year-old," the Cubs team physician said to Toothpick. "His eyes aren't bad with those windows on his face, and his hearing issues shouldn't stop him, but his core is compromised and his back is a ticking time bomb. It's ready to blow any day. I just can't sign him off."

"Excuse me?" Toothpick said with his hands on his hips like an angry parent who *knows* he hasn't heard what he's just heard.

"I can't pass him," the doctor said looking at Toothpick. Then at Wrigley, "He's failed my physical," the doctor calmly said.

"Since when do you need a perfect back to play baseball," Toothpick said.

"I'm just doing my job," the doctor cut him off. "You can go above me."

"Oh you can count on *that*, Doc!" Toothpick said.

Two hours later, Toothpick had gone above the doctor, a little further than he had anticipated. President of Baseball Operations Theo Epstein stood near home plate. Wrigley was on the mound. Four strikeouts later, Theo had a big smile on his face: Happ, Zagunis, Candelario, and Wilson were all out on 16 pitches.

Theo said to Toothpick, "He's in. We'll talk details tomorrow," and walked off toward the tunnel. He stopped, turned around, waved Les over to him, put his arm around his bullpen coach, and whispered, "Call Mark and tell him to keep this kid sharp without overdoing it."

"Mark. Why single A?" asked Les.

"And don't pitch him in a game," Theo said.

"What?" Les said, dumbfounded.

"This guy could be in the show yesterday. But I want to keep him under wraps. We may need a surprise down the stretch…"

"Oh, oh, okay," Les said, with a conspiratorial nod.

★ ★ ★

Two days later, Wrigley was a Kane County Cougar. Just 40 miles away from Wrigley field and his old neighborhood, he was in low-A ball and hoping to make a big splash. But as time went by, he felt like he wasn't going to get a start.

"Coach, can we talk?" Wrigley finally asked his manager.

"Sure."

"I'm not getting any younger, Coach. I'm grateful for getting a contract, but wouldn't you guys like to see what I can do?"

"You'd think so, but I been told to keep you under wraps," said the manager.

"I figured something was up. Why?" Wrigley asked.

"Come here," the manager said, taking Wrigley away from a few players. "I don't want to get too dramatic, but in my 48-plus years of coaching, I've never been part of a conspiracy like this. They don't want the other teams to know about you. And I gotta think it's cause they're going to call you up for the playoffs."

Wrigley just stood there, a little in shock.

"You okay?" asked the crusty old manager.

"I'll be ready," Wrigley said, with a big, toothy grin and sounding eerily like the Terminator.

★ ★ ★

Wrigley's phone rang at 4:00 p.m. on the last day Major League ball clubs were allowed to add players to their post-season roster.

"Hey kid, how's it going?" a man asked

"Uh, who's this?" asked Wrigley.

"Joe," he said. "How's it going?"

"Fine…but, um, I…uh…don't know a Joe."

"Maddon," he laughed. "Joe Maddon. I'm your new skipper."

Wrigley's heart nearly fell out his nether regions. "Joe, c…c…c…coach! I'm…uh…"

"Got some news for ya," Maddon interrupted him. "We're calling you up."

"I'm sorry?" Wrigley said so softly Joe didn't hear him.

"You there?"

"Uh huh."

"Just in the nick too," Maddon said, ignoring Wrigley's confusion, "cause you need to get into a game during the regular season if you're gonna be able to play in the playoffs."

"Wait, you mean, I'm…"

"Don't get too excited. You'll most likely see one batter. And I guarantee they won't let you work your magic. Grab all your gear. You're goin' to Wrigley, Wrigley." Maddon laughed at his own joke. "Goin' to Wrigley, Wrigley," he repeated to himself before hanging up.

CHAPTER 20

The third base coach gave Wrigley the bunt sign. Wrigley looked over toward third and gave him a little nod. It seemed the whole stadium and the millions of people who were watching this World Series knew Wrigley was going to lay down a sacrifice bunt and move the runner into scoring position. The Yankees' third baseman and first basemen both inched in, ready to charge.

The pitcher, knowing that Wrigley was going to bunt, was thinking he'd throw a high fastball right down the pipe. He knew Wrigley couldn't turn on it. He knew this was Wrigley's first ever at bat as a major league baseball player. He knew at worst Wrigley would lay down a bunt right at him; at best, he'd pop the ball up for an easy out or miss it completely.

Wrigley, standing just outside the batter's box, closed his eyes and took a practice swing. Not just any swing, but a near perfect imitation of the Sultan of Swat. It wasn't long ago that Wrigley had spent the day at Tom Smith's emulating Ruth's swing on the stick figure contraption. He had also watched the grainy black and white film of Ruth hitting the fabled home run in Wrigley field. He had practiced, over and over, for hours—the swing, the cadence, the rhythm of Ruth's feet, his bat, how his cleats dug into the ground for leverage. Wrigley dug into the batter's box and pointed to center field. He was calling his shot just like Ruth had, and the crowd stood up, some confused, some in horror, most befuddled.

★ ★ ★

Wrigley arrived five hours before his first game at Wrigley Field and ate an Italian beef sandwich in the left field bleachers—right where he was born. He took a bite, and the mix of sautéed bell peppers, finely chopped carrots, onions, and hot peppers exploded in his mouth. It was a messy sandwich. *A lot like my life*, Wrigley thought. It spilled over his clothes, stained his pants and shirt. He didn't care; it was worth it. He hoped the sting of the hot pepper would linger for hours. His heart raced. His body seemed ready for battle. And now, when he wanted to perform his best, he knew they were going to ask him to refrain from throwing his best stuff. He wanted to blow away the hitters, strike out the side. He would change the course of the game, the season, and get them to the World Series.

"Hey, Wrigley!" yelled the locker manager from the bullpen. "Time to get dressed!"

Wrigley stood up, turned to all four corners of the field, nodding in each direction, just like he had seen his mom do so many times, acknowledging the baseball gods. He looked up at the sky. Big, black clouds were blowing in off the lake. *We'll be lucky to get in a game today*, he thought. He'd seen these kinds of summer storms brewing. They could dump five even ten inches of rain in a few hours. Just as he thought that, the deluge started and didn't let up. Wrigley ran for the lockers. Inside the mixture of damp air, smell of sweaty and stale socks combined to smell like success. He felt like he'd actually been here before. Like he belonged here. He walked along the lockers. *RIZZO, RUSSEL, SANDERS.* His name was scrawled and Scotch-taped, which gave it a pathetic appearance next to the engraved plates on the adjoining lockers, but all he could think was, *I'm a Cub.* Wrigley turned and saw a couple of his teammates—*Yeah, professional Cubbies, his teammates*—looking his way. Anthony Rizzo was finishing getting dressed and gave him a nod and a smile.

"Hey," Rizzo said, "I hear you have some nasty stuff."

"I throw okay," Wrigley said, trying to sound self-deprecating. Rizzo appreciated the gesture and went along with it. "A curveball that drops off the table isn't something *I* want to hit against. The field here stays dry," he went on. "So be ready."

"Kay," Wrigley spat out.

Rizzo turned back to his locker, and Wrigley did the same. Wrigley stood there, for a long, long time, staring at his uniform—a *modern day* Cubs uniform, complete with "Sanders" on the back with the number 88.

He rubbed his fingers over the numbers, thinking how many times he had imagined how this would feel. It was nothing like what he had dreamed. It was better. His mind wandered back to his days on the block, the first time he pitched to Elliott, running down the sidewalk away from the Putney Swope dude, and the river, being at the bottom of the river and seeing the locker—this locker—room. He snapped out of his reverie, looked around, and realized the locker room was deserted. "Crap," Wrigley said. He quickly tied his shoes, and atop his head he placed the *pièce de résistance*—his old-time Cubbie hat.

He jogged through the locker room and out toward the field. Miraculously, the field was in great shape. *Rizzo was right*, he thought as he reached down and touched the grass. *Bone dry.*

Wrigley walked over to Rizzo, who was playing catch with Addison Russell.

"You were right," Wrigley said. Rizzo looked at him curiously. "The field looks perfect."

Rizzo smiled. "What's with the hat?"

Wrigley was confused for a second but then remembered his was not like the others'. "Oh, yeah," he said taking it off and admiring it. "It's my lucky hat. 1908 Cubbies."

"Is it real?" Rizzo asked, surprised like a little kid.

"Oh yeah," said Wrigley, continuing to look it over lovingly. "Beautiful, isn't it?"

"I'll say," Rizzo responded. "Hey, check out that kid over there. He's waving his pen at you."

Wrigley looked to the third base side of the outfield and saw a small boy, about eight or nine, waving a pen in their direction. He was wearing coke-bottle glasses. *Wow*, thought Wrigley, then looking back at Rizzo, "*Really?*"

"Part of the job, rook," said Rizzo, giving him a wink. Wrigley smiled wide and trotted over to the cute kid with curly brown hair standing between his mom and dad. Wrigley couldn't stifle his smile, showing all his crooked teeth as the young man handed him a ball.

"You're blind like me," the kid said.

"Johnny!" said his dad, mortified. "Don't say that—"

"It's okay," Wrigley said nonchalantly. "He's right, I don't see so hot. What's your name, kid?"

"Carl!" he said. "C-A-R-L…"

Wrigley started to sign the ball, momentarily confused about whether he should sign with his left or right hand, then said, "You know what?" He took off his hat and started to write underneath the brim, "To Carl," he said, simultaneously signing—with his left— "Pitch with your heart not your eyes. Best Wishes, Wrigley Sanders." He exaggeratedly affixed the hat on Carl's head, pushing the brim down over his eyes.

Carl laughed. "Thanks, Mr. Sanders!"

"*Wrigley*," replied Wrigley.

"Wrigley," said Carl.

Carl's parents were stunned. "Th…th…thank you, sir," said Carl's mom.

"My pleasure," Wrigley said, continuing to have a chat with Carl for another 5 minutes, talking baseball and ending by telling Carl not to let his poor eyesight limit his vision on life. Finally, with a quick wink goodbye, he jogged back in Rizzo's direction.

"Where's your hat?" Rizzo asked, confused.

Wrigley looked back at Carl. "Someone needed it more than me."

★ ★ ★

Late in the game, when the Cubs were up 10-1, Wrigley got the call from the dugout to warm up.

"You ready?" Les asked.

"Been ready for this since the day I was born," Wrigley said.

Les smiled; he'd heard the story. "Take it easy on these guys tonight. Don't show them any of your fancy pitches. Pitch righty, and no switching."

"All right," Wrigley said disappointedly.

Maddon went to the mound and signaled for Wrigley. Wrigley looked around for the person to whom Joe was signaling and then remembered he was the only one warming up.

"Get on out there, rook!" yelled bullpen catcher Chad Noble.

Wrigley panicked for a second and looked around, confused about where he was. Then he took a deep breath and waddled onto the field. As he approached the mound, his cleat got caught on the lip that separated the infield grass from the mound dirt and he stumbled.

He gathered himself, embarrassed, and dusted himself off. "Easy there, kid," Maddon chuckled putting the ball in his glove. "Remember, no junk."

"Go get 'em, Wrigley," said catcher David Ross, giving Wrigley a pat on the behind with his catcher's mitt.

Ow, Wrigley thought, as Ross jogged back to the plate. He looked around, and through his glasses, squinted to see if he could make out any faces. It was strangely quiet, but everyone seemed to be looking at him like an animal in a zoo.

"Hey!" yelled Ross, "let's warm up."

After eight warm-up pitches—dead, medium-speed fastballs—the umpire turned his head to the man in the on-deck circle and yelled, "Batter up!"

Wrigley pitched to one left-handed hitter, didn't use any of his junk, walked him, and heard boos get louder with each ball.

"Nice pitching, Ducky!" yelled out a drunk, his voice cutting through the crowd.

Maddon made his way out to the mound and held his hand out for the ball. Wrigley dropped his head and dejectedly handed the ball over. "Don't sweat it, Wrigley," he said patting him on the shoulder. "You did exactly what we asked of you—just wait until these folks see what you're *really* made of."

"You'll get 'em next time," Wrigley heard a kid say on his way back to the dugout. Wrigley looked up and saw Carl. When Carl saw Wrigley, he began waving his new old Cubbie hat frantically.

Carl's mom stood behind her son wiggling a bright new custom-made jersey. Wrigley squinted and saw that it read, "SANDERS." Wrigley smiled as he made his way down the steps, his new teammates all giving him a pat. He took a seat right next to Jake Arrieta, hoping some of his magic just might rub off on him.

The next morning, Wrigley awoke to a storm bigger than the one that had blown in the night before. He nearly spit out his coffee when he saw, right on the front page of the local papers, photos of Wrigley with his 1908 hat, handing it over to Carl, signing it, with headlines that were sure to give Theo Epstein heartburn.

"*Mystery player predicts Cubs will take the World Series this year.*"

"*'You can do anything you want to do,' he promised the kid.*"

"*He's blind, deaf...the Cubs' new secret weapon!*"

The last headline made Theo throw up in his mouth. Arthur Bornstein, the PR person Theo called into his office, told him in a measured tone, "Just send him back down. It'll blow over in a day or two. Everybody will forget about him. He didn't show anything on the mound yesterday."

★ ★ ★

Nestled in her den, Bubbs became frantic—at least for a 108-year-old. She made a surplus of pitcher dolls that started to pile up on her TV trays.

"Don't stand a chance," Wrigley joked, looking at the piles of dolls during a short visit home.

"Going all the way with that kind of help," Biggs told Bubbs.

She grinned, gums and all—a single tooth hanging on for dear life. Her body was becoming frailer by the day, and both Wrigley and Biggs looked at each other in silence, hoping she would hold out for the playoffs.

"Come here, you two," Bubbs weakly barked out. Biggs and Wrigley came closer. "Remember how Sandy always said to pitch inside?" She shot a steely look at Wrigley.

"Yes ma'am" said Wrigley, caught in her earnest stare.

"I think it's time you learned 'bout 'Chinski,'" she said.

"Who?" Biggs asked.

"Root," said Bubbs, "Charlie Root."

"Cubs all-time leader in wins and innings pitched," Wrigley proudly said.

"Did you know they called him 'Chinski' cause he pitched high and inside to hitters crowding the plate?" she said.

"Hadn't heard that," Wrigley said.

"Doesn't always work," she said. "October 1, during the 1932 World Series. Sit down, you two. Sit down."

The boys complied, sitting cross-legged right in front of her rocker, listening like little children.

"Back in '32, in the fifth inning of the third game of the series, tied 4 to 4, Babe Ruth came up to bat against Root. He was playing in his tenth and last World Series. They were playing at Wrigley, and the fans were giving Ruth a hard time. Hell, he's a Yankee, why not right? The Babe was in full form. So was Root. The first pitch was a called strike. Ruth looked over at the Cubbie dugout, raised his right hand and extended one of his fingers."

"He flipped them off?" Biggs asked.

"His *index finger*, Biggs" said Bubbs. The next two pitches were balls. Finally, Root blasted a fastball right down the pipe for a called second strike. The crowd went wild. Apparently, so did the Cubs dugout. They said a lot of nasty stuff to Ruth, who waved two fingers to the Cubs dugout, told Root a thing or two. Nobody but Root knows what he said, but it wasn't, "Let's go out for coffee."

Bubbs went on, "Two and two, then Ruth pointed, right toward the fences. Some say he was predicting a home run off the Cubs' all-time leader in wins and innings pitched. Root tried to fool him with a curveball, but Ruth put it over the deepest part of centerfield. That ball flew 490 feet. The famous 'called shot' that everyone *still* talks about. The damn Yankees went on to sweep us in four games."

Wrigley had heard this story before—it was one of Grandpa Connor's favorites—but Bubbs lent her own brand of enthusiasm, and Wrigley loved it.

He feigned a look of surprise to give her encouragement.

"I know!" said Bubbs in response to Wrigley's look. "They kept Root in the game, and on the very next pitch, Lou Gehrig hit a homer into the right field seats."

"*Really?*" responded Wrigley, for whom this bit about Gehrig was new news.

"Yes, I was there!" she said pointing a bony finger at her chest. "What bothers me is why didn't Root throw high and inside to Ruth, get him off the plate." Then she smiled, leaned back in her chair, and promptly fell asleep. She was most likely done for the day.

But she had sparked an interest in the Ruth/Root encounter in Wrigley. He promptly went home and played the footage. It was in black and white, of course, and rather grainy, but he watched as Ruth held up one finger, then another to the dugout, and finally, pointed toward Root, or the fence, depending on your particular interpretation of the event. Wrigley stayed up almost all night, like he used to in the old days, studying the film. The next day he even stick-figured Root's windup with

Tom Smith, and just for the fun of it, stick-figured Ruth's swing and went home and practiced it for hours. *You never know,* thought Wrigley, *I may actually get up to bat.*

CHAPTER 21

George, Monty Jack, Work, Mary Jane Smith, and most of the neighbors were watching the World Series game with Bubbs in the den on Lasaine Street.

"Wrigs is gonna swing for the fences!" said Bubbs, excited.

"Bubbs," Regina said, rolling her eyes, "even I know Wrigs is gonna lay down a bunt. The whole world knows!"

But Bubbs had a Wrigley baseball card Biggs had made for her. A real one didn't exist, so Biggs had to resort to the magic of Photoshop. She was rubbing it and chanting something about Babe Ruth. Most everyone in the room just rolled their eyes and looked back at the TV.

★ ★ ★

After pointing his bat like the Babe, Wrigley felt a little silly. What had gotten into him? He wasn't a showboat, even though that kind of behavior was more acceptable and commonplace in modern-day baseball. He hoped he could at least move the runner over to second. One thing he was certain of was that if he tapped into his inner Sultan of Swat, things would work out all right. *This was one heck of a dream*, he thought. *Why not?*

The ball came rushing right down the center of the plate at close to 95 miles an hour. Wrigley, to his credit, started his swing early. But he wasn't a major league hitter, so his bat didn't get through the zone quick enough to pull the ball to the right side, but he did pull off his best imitation of Ruth, even lifting up his left heel at the end of his swing. The bat hit the ball, which traveled toward left field, low at first, then rising higher and higher.

The Yankees' left fielder didn't even take a step, it was headed right toward him, but Chicago's famous winds kept blowing the ball higher and longer.

The roar was so loud even Wrigley's new hearing aids had a hard time adjusting to it. He stood in the batter's box, knowing that he'd hit the ball—that he'd hit it hard—but he couldn't see where the damn thing went. And it never occurred to him to actually run.

Wrigley squinted toward left field and saw the left field umpire with his arm up in the air twirling his hand around signifying a home run.

Wait, thought Wrigley, *no...*

Wrigley, unsure about what to do, looked behind the plate, awaiting home plate umpire Kent Murphy's instructions. But Murphy just stood right next to Yankee catcher Brian McCann, identical statues, masks atop their heads staring out at the left field bleachers.

"Blue?" asked Wrigley.

Murphy looked at Wrigley, who just stood there looking back at him. He shrugged his shoulders and said, "Game ain't over 'til you cross the plate, kid."

Wrigley came out of his trance and realized what was happening. He didn't want a repeat of "Merkle's Boner." He needed to cross the plate. Wrigley started walking tentatively toward first base, then jogging. Then he raised his arms above his head as he confidently waddled around the bases, Yankee players and field umpires all continuing to stare out into the left field bleachers in complete disbelief.

"I thought I'd seen it all," said Vinny from the booth. "Folks, this is the most magical moment these eyes have ever witnessed. Listen to the crowd, folks. Listen to the crowd."

His teammates were waiting for him as Wrigley crossed home plate. They scooped him up and carried him around the infield, high above their heads. Wrigley felt like he was floating. He tore off his shirt, waving it in the air, revealing his white upper body covered with his huge Cubs tattoo that wrapped around his chest and back…everyone in the stadium saw him on the monitor and the stadium went ballistic.

Black Patty and half the crew from the boiler room had made the trip all the way from L.A. They were in right field and looked like a cross breed of punk rockers, freaks, and out-of-work actors, mostly because they were. They spelled out "W-r-i-g-l-e-y" on large placards and flipped them as Wrigley came past the right field bleachers.

He looked out over the crowd behind the third baseline, and for a moment swore he saw Bubbs walking out of the stadium up the stairs, carrying a black cat. Next to her were Billy

Cianis and his goat Murphy, and right next to Murphy walked Steve Bartman.

Wrigley just stared at them as they coasted up the stairs. Then, just before they left the stadium, they started to fade away—first, Billy and his goat, then the black cat, then Bartman, and finally, with a big grin on her face, Bubbs waved to Wrigley and slowly disappeared from the stairs. Wrigley felt his body gently being lowered to the ground from the players' shoulders, and a sports broadcaster snapped him out of his reverie by asking him "How did it feel to hit the game winning home run?"

Wrigley turned and looked back just above the Cubs' dug out. He swore he saw Sandy Koufax sitting amongst all the ghosts of Wrigley's past. *How would you answer that question?*

Wrigley turned to the sports broadcaster and said, "It's Cubs' baseball. Anything can happen!" and looked up toward his Papa.